ALIBI FOR A JUDGE

Mr Justice Carstairs is not a good judge because he worries about his cases. Having sentenced a man to ten years' imprisonment he suddenly gets pangs of conscience about the way he conducted the trial. With the help of the young wife of the convicted man, he sets out to prove his innocence, only to become convinced that he was plainly guilty. The judge is now in a far worse predicament, for he has to consider whether he has not in fact been led up the garden by an attractive young female blackmailer.

HENRY CECIL

★

Alibi for a Judge

London
MICHAEL JOSEPH

First published by
MICHAEL JOSEPH LTD
26 *Bloomsbury Street*
*London, W.C.*1
MARCH 1960
SECOND IMPRESSION MAY 1960
THIRD IMPRESSION JULY 1966

Reproduced & printed offset litho in Great Britain
by The Hollen Street Press Ltd., London, W.1.

CONTENTS

1	On Alibis	7
2	On Judges	11
3	Trial	20
4	Verdict	32
5	Retrospect	43
6	Interview with a Judge	47
7	Court of Criminal Appeal	55
8	At the Home Office	60
9	Unusual Conference	67
10	The Views of Brothers in Law	77
11	Under Starter's Orders	82
12	They're Off	90
13	Mr Routang at Home	95
14	A Capture	101
15	Unusual Interview	107
16	To Write or not to Write	110
17	On Holiday	113
18	Interruptions to a Holiday	124
19	The Last Chance	128
20	Mr Thompson Again	145
21	Interview with a Headmaster	154
22	A Plain Case of Fraud	169
23	The Problem	174
24	Under Caution	181
25	Extraordinary	190
26	The Headmaster Again	196
27	Back to Work	205

CHAPTER ONE

On Alibis

WILLIAM BURFORD's defence was an alibi and the judge who presided at his trial was Mr Justice Carstairs. The alibi was not one of the best alibis and the judge was not one of the best judges. It may perhaps help to an understanding of the case and its curious consequences to consider first the nature of an alibi and then the nature of a judge.

From time immemorial the alibi as a defence has been popular with criminals. And not only with criminals. Most people remember Mr Weller senior's despairing cry, 'Oh, Sammy, Sammy, Vy worn't there a alleybi?' when Mrs Bardell won her action against Mr Pickwick. It is logical enough. The charge against William Burford was safe breaking on a pretty large scale. It was alleged that, with the help of another or others, he had not only blown open the safe but removed about £80,000 as well. No doubt William said to himself: 'If I can prove I was elsewhere when the safe was blown, I'm bound to be acquitted.' And he was quite right; it was a cast-iron defence—if it succeeded.

That is the trouble with alibis. They are at the same time the best and worst defences. They are the best because, if you weren't there when the man was murdered, you couldn't have murdered him. They are the worst because, once you raise an alibi, no other defence is usually open to you. In the case of murder, for example, you can't rely on self-defence, accident or extreme

7

provocation. You say you weren't there. So you can't have been provoked; you can't have been threatened by the man and picked up a weapon with which to defend yourself; he can't have slipped on a piece of orange skin and fallen accidentally on to the knife with which you were peeling the orange. You were nowhere near the man at the time. Or so you say. And, if the jury don't believe you, that's an end of the matter.

Criminal cases are not like civil cases in this respect. Judges and barristers are quite used to inconsistent and alternative defences in civil matters. Says the plaintiff in the County Court:

'Your Honour, the defendant owes me £50 for goods sold and delivered.'

'What do you say?' says the judge to the defendant.

'Oh, your Honour,' says the defendant, 'I never agreed to buy the goods.'

'An excellent defence,' says the judge. 'Any other?'

'Oh, yes, your Honour. He never delivered them to me.'

'Better and better,' says the judge. 'Any more?'

'Oh, yes, your Honour. They were no good and I couldn't re-sell them.'

'Yes,' says the judge. 'What's the next one?'

'He agreed to take them back.'

'Fine,' says the judge, 'and now he refuses to do so?'

'Exactly, your Honour,' says the defendant. 'And I've one further defence.'

'I felt sure of it,' says the judge. 'Keep the best till the last. What is it?'

'I've paid for them, your Honour.'

'As I thought,' says the judge. 'How many children have you got?'

'Five, your Honour.'

'Very well, then. Pay £2 a month.'

Well, perhaps it isn't quite like that, though, according to a current story, that is how it seemed to an American lawyer who was visiting the English Courts.

But, though this sort of thing can be done in a civil court, where the only issue is usually whether A should pay B and, if so, how much and when, it is quite impossible in a criminal court. For example, in William's case it was alleged that he was seen running from the scene of the crime. Having sworn that at the time he was some miles away in bed with his wife, it would have been impossible for him to rely alternatively on the inconsistent defence that he was a customer of the bank and he had gone to sleep while waiting in a queue of people all of whom were paying in vast numbers of cheques and notes, which had to be counted and re-counted; that, when the bank closed, he was somehow or other forgotten and locked in; that he was disturbed by the real thieves, that when he realised the position, he thought he might find himself in a compromising situation if he remained and so he bolted down the street. Nor, if that story seems anyway rather fantastic, could he have said more simply, as an alternative to his alibi, that he was certainly seen running from the scene but that it was a pure coincidence; he happened to be in the neighbourhood at the time and was in a hurry to get home.

No, once you've committed yourself to an alibi, that is your only mode of escape, and, if that breaks down, you must wait, as composedly as you can, for the sentence. In consequence the wise criminal thinks carefully before he relies on an alibi. And the wisest prepare it in advance, as in a military operation, with watches synchronised and excellent reasons arranged for the supporters of his alibi being able to remember the time when the accused was supposed to have been with them. Up to midnight the wireless is a most useful asset. The supporter listens to the programme and (provided the accused doesn't get arrested on the spot) primes him with it later.

Many people are rather sceptical of alibis and, indeed, some cynics say that they are never genuine. They argue that, if the accused really was somewhere else at the time the crime was committed, he would never have been charged with it. But this implies that no innocent person is ever charged with crime, and, though it is a very rare occurrence, it does occasionally happen. William passionately declared that it had happened in his case.

CHAPTER TWO

On Judges

IT should perhaps help to an understanding of Mr Justice Carstairs' behaviour after the trial of William Burford to have some appreciation of a judge's position in England.

How are they appointed, what qualities do they require to make them satisfactory judges, how and why do some of them fail to be satisfactory and what is the effect upon themselves and upon the public of such failure?

Mr Justice Carstairs had been appointed in the normal way, that is to say, he had had a substantial practice at the Bar, was looked upon as a sound lawyer and a person of complete integrity; he was offered the appointment by the Lord Chancellor, and he accepted. There was no surprise at his appointment and no expectation that he would either be very good or very bad.

In some countries there is a judges' profession and, if you want to become a judge, rather than an advocate, you must join that profession. If you do join it, you no doubt start off in some administrative capacity with no judicial duties, but you see how the judges do their work. Then, in due course, you will be given some very minor judicial post, and your progress thereafter will presumably depend upon how you acquit yourself in that post and in any more important posts which you may be given.

The result is that no one in those countries is appointed to high judicial office unless he has proved himself to possess not only the qualities necessary for a good judge but the ability to make full use of those qualities as well. In consequence, the public in those countries can be almost certain that, unless the extra power suddenly goes to a man's head, the judge holding high judicial office will be patient and fair-minded, intelligent, a good lawyer and, perhaps most important of all, not an advocate on the Bench. It can also be reasonably sure that he will not be a person who worries excessively. No one can, of course, be quite certain of that matter, as a judge may carry on his worrying entirely in private and never disclose it to any superiors, colleagues or subordinates, but this does not often happen.

It is, of course, possible that preferment to high judicial office will suddenly go to a man's head, but, if he has been having continuous preferment for many years, it is fairly certain that he is not a person whom power corrupts.

The position of a High Court judge in England is extremely important and there is, therefore, obviously something to be said for ensuring that no one is appointed to that office unless he has proved himself to be fitted for it. A man may be a brilliant lawyer and a brilliant advocate and an appallingly bad judge. And you cannot tell for certain what sort of a judge he will make until he is on the Bench. If a mistake has been made, it is then too late to correct it.

In spite of this danger the English system of the appointment of judges entirely from the Bar has worked, on the whole, extremely satisfactorily, but undoubtedly it has fallen down from time to time. It was a mistake to appoint Mr Justice Carstairs, though neither he nor anyone else realised it at the time. But the advantage of the system is that the judge, having been at the Bar most of his working life, understands all that has been happening before the case comes into Court and all that is happening from the advocate's point of view in Court. This knowledge is of the greatest value and is only available to judges in those countries where they are appointed from the Bar.

The one case where the English system has in the past been known quite unnecessarily to fail has been in the appointment of the Lord Chief Justice. His position is of the greatest importance, both to the judges and to the public, but until comparatively recently there was a practice by which he was appointed direct from the Bar, the Attorney-General of the day being considered to have some kind of moral right to be so appointed. The strong probability is that this practice is now defunct and that no Lord Chief Justice of England will ever be appointed except from among the judges themselves. It would seem elementary that no one should be appointed to such high office unless he has proved that he is a judge of the highest quality. The unfortunate result of appointing as Lord Chief Justice an Attorney-General, who was a man of brilliant ability in many respects but whose judicial qualities had never been tested, and were in fact dreadfully deficient, is well within the memory of many lawyers, and it is unlikely that such a risk will ever be taken again. It was necessary to take a risk in appointing Mr Justice Carstairs a judge of the Queen's Bench Division. It would have been ludicrous to take the risk of making him Lord Chief Justice. How ludicrous this story will show.

No little handbook entitled *Do's and Don'ts for Judges* is issued to barristers on their appointment to the Bench. Most of them realise instinctively what is required of them. Even those who do not turn out to be particularly good judges try to act as particularly good judges do act. This has the advantage that on the whole litigants feel that justice has been done, even if it hasn't, and apparent justice is the next best thing to justice itself. Nor do newly-appointed judges attend a short course of lectures with the object of receiving helpful advice from their more experienced brethren.

All the same, a class for new judges is a pleasant idea.

'Now, Toothcombe J., what would you do in a case where the plaintiff said, etc., etc.?'

Toothcombe J. remains deep in thought.

'Come along, Toothcombe J., one of the things a judge has to do is to make up his mind.'

Still no answer.

'Very well then. Next. Next. Next. I see your hand is up, Blinkers J. What is your answer to the problem?'

'I was just stretching, I'm afraid.'

'Oh, very well. So long as it was a genuine yawn, I don't think it matters very much. But never do it on purpose.'

But, although handbooks and lectures are quite unnecessary for the average judge, it would have been a good thing if Mr Justice Carstairs could have had the advantage of both. For, although in private life he was a kindly and generous man, he was one of the few judges who did not appreciate instinctively his responsibilities, or realise how easy it was to abuse the power vested in him.

An omnibus conductor has considerable authority in his omnibus. He can't tell people to take their hands out of their pockets or to stop sucking sweets but he can order people about to a substantial extent. Few conductors abuse this power but some do. Such abuses cannot do much harm, although they can start an unfortunate train of events moving. If a conductor is rude to a business man, it may rankle until he reaches his office. He may find there that a clerk has made a mistake. Normally he would have overlooked it, but, unconsciously, in order to be avenged for the conductor's rudeness, he creates a fuss about it all and makes some unwarranted remarks to the clerk. Eventually the clerk is provoked into answering back and is given a week's notice. This may lead to all sorts of domestic complications.

'Lost your job, have you? What am I going to use for housekeeping, tell me that?'

'It wasn't my fault, really, Mary.'

No, it wasn't. It was the conductor's.

So, even the abuse of authority on that very small scale

can have serious effects. And, conversely, good manners and helpful conduct, even on a small scale, can start a chain reaction of a happier kind.

But abuse of power by a judge may very well have serious effects. It is one thing for a man to be told in public to get off an omnibus, it is quite another for a judge to say of him in public, with the probability that it will be reported in the press:

'I have never seen such a nauseating spectacle as Mr X in the witness box. He is incapable of telling the truth except when it suits him and he tells his lies in a sanctimonious and self-righteous manner which I find utterly repulsive.'

When Mr Justice Carstairs, on his way home from Court, read in the newspaper '*Mr X . . . a nauseating spectacle*. Judge,' he entirely failed to appreciate that in speaking of Mr X in that way he had simply satisfied his own personal dislike of the man. For the purposes of his decision it was quite unnecessary for him to do more than to say that he did not accept Mr X's evidence and why: for example, that some of his evidence was contrary to letters which he had written or that he contradicted himself in the witness box or the like. But to describe him as a nauseating hypocrite was to indulge in mere abuse. Perhaps the judge was right in this view, perhaps he was not, but, though his judgment could be reversed in a higher Court, his words could never become unspoken.

And, after all, he had seen the man in the box for perhaps an hour. It may be that in the unaccustomed atmosphere of the Court Mr X went to pieces and did not do himself justice. It is indeed surprising that so many witnesses are able to control themselves sufficiently to appear outwardly calm. Justice can never be perfect and, if a man is a bad witness, he may lose his case, but he should not have to suffer the sort of treatment which Mr Justice Carstairs handed out. And unfortunately no one who knew the judge well enough ever told him of this defect in his behaviour. It was as bad as that of a judge who said to an acquitted prisoner:

'You're discharged. You're very lucky in your jury.'

In saying that, the judge had endeavoured to cast doubt upon the jury's verdict in order to satisfy his own sense of annoyance at the prisoner being acquitted.

A further serious fault of Mr Justice Carstairs was his complete inability to restrain himself from intervening during the course of a case. Everyone knows the man who can't refrain from taking the lead in private conversation. If a story, which he happens to know, is being told, he can't resist interrupting and finishing it off. So with Mr Justice Carstairs in Court. It has frequently been said that a judge should hold himself aloof from the struggle going on in Court between the advocates. Of course sometimes he has to blow his whistle when there has been an infringe-ment of the rules, or when someone has been hurt, but otherwise he should leave the battle to the advocates. Mr Justice Carstairs, however, girded himself for war and joined lustily in the fight.

Another of his serious faults was to have carried his advocacy to the Bench. That is one of the prices of the system of appointing judges solely from advocates. But it is impossible to tell whether a man will do this until you see him at work on the Bench. It by no means follows that, because a man has been a fierce and determined advocate, he will not be completely fair-minded on the Bench. One even finds such an advocate, on appointment to the Bench, having difficulty in coming to a decision. But the judge who carries his advocacy to the Bench makes up his mind (often much too early) as to what in his opinion the result of the case should be and proceeds to press that point of view, just as though he were the advocate whose duty it was to press it. A judge cannot help forming a view about a case as it goes on; that is what he is there for. But, as far as possible, he should keep it to himself and in no circum-

stances should he try to steer the case to the result which
he considers it should have. A judge who apparently
seems to procure a particular result in a case must
invariably appear unfair.

It was unfortunate that Mr Justice Carstairs should
have these faults but by themselves they would only have
resulted in his being a bad judge. It was the combination
of these faults with two other faults which caused him to
act so strangely. He was a worrier and he indulged in
self-deception.

It is important for a judge, both for his own peace of
mind and for the quality of his decisions, that he should
not worry about them. He should do his very best to get
them right, but, having done so and delivered his judgments, he should not be tormented by doubts about their
correctness. A judge should be able to make up his mind
and, having done so, he should give his decision and go to
the theatre.

There was once a judge who had many admirable
judicial qualities but he worried so much about his cases
that he actually died within a comparatively short time
of his appointment, because his mind and body could not
stand the strain any more. Mr Justice Carstairs did not
die from worry but this can only have been because his
mind and body were both able to stand the strain better
than the judge who died. But he tormented himself
unmercifully when he had any doubt about a decision he
had given.

He also indulged in self-deception. Most young
barristers have done this in their early days. The young
man loses a case in a County Court, and on his way back
from the trial suddenly thinks of something which he
failed to do and which might have altered the whole
situation. For a moment he feels quite sick, and then he
starts to convince himself either that his new idea was not
in fact a good one, or that it would really have made no
difference if he had put it into effect. Before he has got

back to chambers he has decided that no one else could have won the case, although in his heart of hearts he knows this is not true. Most young men grow out of this habit, and start to learn to profit by their mistakes. They still find on the way back from Court that they've forgotten to ask an essential question or something of that kind, but they no longer try to convince themselves that it would have made no difference. In other words they seek to profit from holding a post-mortem and they resolve to try to do better in the future.

In its strict sense an alibi means a claim that you were elsewhere at the time something happened. But the word is also used loosely and inaccurately to mean simply an excuse. In that sense Mr Justice Carstairs had from the start of his career at the Bar used alibis and on his way home from Court, after having given judgment in a rather difficult case, he would suddenly think of some point that he thought he might have overlooked. Thereupon the worrying side of his mind and his power of self-deception would have a fine struggle and by the time he reached home he would have decided that he was right after all. That, however, would not prevent him from having a very bad night through worrying about it all over again.

But for the explanation of how judges are appointed readers might have wondered how this particular judge came to be appointed. But he was quite a good lawyer and some of the faults which made him unqualified to be a judge were not appreciated when he was only an advocate. They were not even appreciated by the judge himself. Had they been, he would never have accepted the offer. There is a considerable strain on a judge imposed by the mere concentration which he has to maintain throughout the case. But, if he has serious difficulty in coming to a conclusion on any but the simplest cases, and if he continually worries after most of his decisions and is only stopped by having to concentrate on the next case, the burden is too great for him.

A man once said to a judge:

'If you make that order I shall commit suicide.'

The judge made the order and the man committed suicide. Had such an event occurred to Mr Justice Carstairs he might conceivably have committed suicide himself, but, even if he had refrained from taking that drastic step, he would have undergone torments. In fact the judge had no alternative but to make the order. He reported the threat to all the responsible authorities and there was no more that he could do. If a judge were to yield in any way to such a threat, any litigant could win his case by making it, as no one could ever tell whether he really meant it. Of course it wouldn't last very long with that particular judge, as very soon both sides would make the same threat and it would become common form for counsel for the plaintiff, having asked all the relevant questions material to the case, to add this last one before sitting down:

'And now, Mr Y, will you kindly tell the learned judge what you will do if he does not decide in your favour?'

'I shall commit suicide.'

'Thank you, Mr Y. That is all I have to ask.'

Then counsel for the defendant would do exactly the same and the threats would pretty well cancel out. Of course it might be awkward when there was a claim and a counter-claim and the judge dismissed them both. No doubt in such a case he would warn both plaintiff and defendant that it would be a serious contempt of Court to put their threat into practice within the precincts of the Court.

Fortunately for William Burford he had no idea of the nature of the judge who was going to try him. He had indeed asked his counsel what the judge was like and had received the assurance:

'Don't you worry about the judge. It's the jury that matters.'

CHAPTER THREE

Trial

I T was more comforting for William to be told that than to be told: 'He's the very devil and will get you convicted if he possibly can.'

And that was the only reason that William's counsel, Mr Empton, said what he did. He was an able and experienced practitioner in the Criminal Courts and he knew perfectly well that in a difficult case, like William's, he would have the judge against him. It follows from what has been said earlier that a judge should not be 'against' anyone when a man is being tried by a jury. And, even when he is trying a civil case alone, he should not appear to be against either side until he gives his judgment. But Mr Empton knew well that, unless he were extremely lucky, Mr Justice Carstairs would run the case against him from start to finish, and that, though the verdict would be the jury's, it might well be difficult for them in a case of this kind to withstand the pressure from the Bench. But there was no point in worrying his client unduly in advance by telling him this. He had enough to worry about as it was.

It is well known among lawyers that, when something starts to go wrong with a case, it often happens that nearly everything seems to go wrong. Usually, though not quite always, this is because the case is a bad one. William's case began badly and got worse as it went on. It started with a bad judge, it was dependent on a poor alibi, something happened in the course of the case which made the alibi even worse, and throughout the case the judge and

Mr Empton were at loggerheads. William soon became like a passenger on a sinking ship. The captain (Empton) was on the bridge doing his best but the waves were battering the boat unmercifully, it was taking in water all the time and, though, of course, a rescue was always possible, it appeared to William at almost every stage of the trial that he was going down. The captain, of course, would not have to go down with his ship.

The first witness against William was a policeman. At about 11. 30 p.m. he had been on beat duty near a branch of a well-known bank when he heard what sounded like a muffled explosion. He stopped and listened but heard nothing more, and saw nothing. He thought it must have been the sound of a collision in the distance. After standing still for a minute or two, he continued on his beat. About twenty minutes later he heard a sound of someone running. Turning round a corner he saw a man running and carrying a suitcase. He called on him to stop. The man glanced round and increased his pace. The policeman followed, but lost him. Later he identified William as the man he had seen.

Mr Empton had a difficult decision to make when he rose to cross-examine the policeman. The witness had admittedly only seen the man's face for a moment, but he had unquestionably picked him out at an identification parade. As far as William could tell, this parade was a perfectly fair one. But—and it was a very big but—some eight years previously William had unfortunately served a sentence of six months imprisonment for receiving goods knowing them to have been stolen. Since his release from prison he had apparently gone straight. He had married a charming girl and taken a steady job and, as far as was known, had avoided the bad company he had been keeping at the time of his conviction.

In consequence of this conviction, however, the police had a photograph of William. If the witness had been shown this photograph before the identification it would be easy enough for him to pick out William. It might have been shown to him perfectly properly with other photographs, *before* William's arrest, to see if he could spot the man. On the other hand, it might have been shown to him *after* William's arrest, in an excess of zeal by the police who, believing that William was their man, wanted to secure a conviction. On the whole it was most unlikely that it was shown to the witness before the arrest, as William had never been concerned in safe blowing or anything of that sort. But Mr Empton's difficulty was that any cross-examination by him to suggest that the witness had seen a photograph of the accused might very well lead an intelligent member of the jury to realise that William had a previous conviction for crime. Mr Empton did not consider that this was one of those rare cases where it was desirable to rely upon the fact that the accused had a criminal record, and accordingly he was in a dilemma. The policeman positively identified William. It was no use simply shouting at him that he was a liar or asking if he had made a mistake. The policeman would politely deny such suggestions. On the other hand, the only method of making an inroad on the identification was by referring to a matter which might gravely prejudice his client's chances of acquittal. He also had to bear in mind that, if the witness had been deliberately shown a photograph of William before the parade, it was most unlikely that he would admit it. So that all he might get for his pains would be a statement that there was such a photograph in existence—which would be a pointer to a previous conviction—and a denial that the policeman had ever seen it.

Such a situation requires the most delicate handling and even the most brilliant and intelligent advocate might take a wrong course or come to grief when taking the right one. Mr Empton's cross-examination went as follows:

EMPTON: You only caught a glimpse of his face, Officer?

WITNESS: I saw it, sir.

EMPTON: I know you saw it, but it was only for a moment, wasn't it?

WITNESS: It was only for a moment but I saw it plainly.

EMPTON: Have you a good memory for faces?

WITNESS: Average, I suppose, sir.

EMPTON: You didn't see the prisoner in the police station until five days after you saw the man running?

WITNESS: That is correct.

EMPTON: Had you been trying to memorise his face in the meantime?

WITNESS: Yes, sir, I had.

EMPTON: How d'you do that?

WITNESS: Well, I just did it, sir. It struck me as very suspicious that a man carrying a suitcase refused to stop when called upon by me, and I tried to keep his face in mind.

EMPTON: Not an easy thing to do?

WITNESS: I don't know, sir. I've never really tried to do it before.

EMPTON: When did you first give information about this man?

WITNESS: I reported it immediately on the telephone, sir. And later that night, when I heard of the bank robbery, I made a further report.

EMPTON: Did you have any difficulty in identifying the accused at the parade?

WITNESS: I had to look along the line of men twice, sir, and then I felt sure.

EMPTON: Did you have any help in identifying him?

JUDGE: What d'you mean—have any help?

EMPTON: My Lord, I would respectfully ask your Lordship to allow me to ask the question without intervening.

JUDGE: But the jury and the witness and I must know what you mean by the question. You say 'did he have help?' Help could be given in a variety of ways.

EMPTON: My Lord, I'm sure your Lordship must

realise the difficulties which counsel sometimes have in this type of cross-examination.

JUDGE: Some cases are very difficult.

EMPTON: My Lord, I do most respectfully protest at that observation, and I ask for a new trial before a fresh jury.

JUDGE: Certainly not. Go on with your cross-examination.

EMPTON: Well, Officer, did you have any help?

JUDGE: What d'you mean by 'help'? Do you mean— was the prisoner pointed out to the witness before he went on the parade? Is that what you mean? I'll ask the officer myself. Did that happen, Officer?

WITNESS: No, my Lord.

JUDGE: Is that what you meant, Mr Empton?

EMPTON: No, my Lord.

JUDGE: Then kindly explain what you do mean.

EMPTON: I wish your Lordship would let me ask the question.

JUDGE: It's no good you asking the question unless the witness knows what it means. Do you know what it means, Officer?

WITNESS: No, my Lord.

It would have taken a particularly scrupulous and courageous policeman to reply to that last question: 'Yes, perfectly, my Lord.' Whether such a witness would have become a Chief Constable, Commissioner of Police, or have eventually been dismissed as unsuitable for the police force, is a matter for conjecture.

So Mr Empton's difficulties, which were very great anyway, were increased by the judge. Before he started his cross-examination he had thought for a moment that he had a brainwave. His client was not an athlete but he had done a little running, and Mr Empton had ascertained that a picture of him had once appeared in a local paper when he was running with the Loamshire Harriers. Mr Empton considered a cross-examination on these lines: 'Now, Officer,' he thought of saying, 'my client has

done a certain amount of running and has had his picture
in the papers. I suppose you hadn't by any chance seen
a photograph of my client before the identification
parade?'

Mr Empton felt he could rely on the witness playing
the game. The police know all about the danger of a
prisoner's past bad character being made known to the
jury, and never voluntarily refer to it. Mr Empton felt
that he and the police officer could have a complete
understanding about what he meant by a photograph, but
the jury would have been misled (though, for once,
perfectly properly) by the reference to the local paper.

At first, when Mr Empton had, without much hope,
enquired of his client whether he had ever had his picture
in the paper, he had been delighted at the reply, but he
eventually decided it was not worth it. To pray in aid that
the accused was a bit of a runner when it was alleged that
he had outrun the police officer, seemed tantamount to
suicide.

So Mr Empton continued cross-examining the witness
as best he could, having regard to the actual difficulties
of the situation, increased as they were by the interruptions
of the judge. And Mr Justice Carstairs did not simply
interfere with his mouth. He interfered with his eyes,
which turned towards the jury with a look which said
pretty plainly:

'I'm sorry, members of the jury, that your time has to
be wasted like this. But that is one of the misfortunes of
our present situation which we each have to bear. This
man is obviously guilty but we have to humour the public
conscience, which likes to go through the motions of
trying him.'

In other words Mr Justice Carstairs indulged in all the
tricks of the lesser and least judges, who, entirely forgetful
of the true role they should be playing, deliberately try to
steer a case in the direction which they themselves think
it should take. Although they know perfectly well that the

verdict should be the jury's they do all they can to see that that verdict shall coincide with their opinion. Occasionally, even, they are hypocritical enough to say something like this:

'Members of the jury, the verdict in this case is yours and yours alone. And, if you think that inadvertently I have expressed my own opinion, you should entirely disregard it unless it happens to coincide with your own.'

Such advice, given genuinely when a judge has not acted as Mr Justice Carstairs was acting, is sound and fair enough—and often given by judges of the highest distinction. It is only when it is said by a judge who has deliberately tried to procure the verdict he wants that it is objectionable.

That Mr Justice Carstairs should form an opinion during the case was only to be expected. No one with the intelligence of a judge, however mediocre, listening attentively to the whole of the evidence in a case, could fail to do so. But he should have kept his opinion to himself. It is true enough that 99 out of every 100 people who stand in the dock are guilty, but, if one is to take account of that fact, one might as well give up trying them altogether, and explain to the luckless 1 per cent that it is far cheaper to convict everyone and that they are suffering in the cause of the national economy.

It is important to bear these considerations in mind. Otherwise it might be difficult to appreciate the extraordinary behaviour of Mr Justice Carstairs after the trial.

After Mr Empton had unsuccessfully tried to attack the evidence of the police officer he sat down. There was no re-examination and the next witness was called. This was a detective-sergeant who, in company with another police officer, had called on William five days after the robbery. The effect of his evidence was this. As a result of information given to him, he went to the house where William lived with his attractive wife, Lesley. The detective-sergeant did not state that she was attractive but later she came into Court and everyone could see it for themselves.

William had opened the door to the officers and had seemed very ill at ease when they told him who they were.

'Mr Burford,' the sergeant had said, 'are you prepared to tell us where you were at 11 p.m. on the 23rd of this month?'

William had thought for a moment and then said that he had gone for an hour's walk, as he did not feel sleepy enough.

'By yourself?'

'Yes.'

'So no one can confirm your story?'

'My wife can say I went out.'

'But she can't prove where you went?'

'No, of course not.'

'D'you mind if we look round your flat?'

William had hesitated. Eventually:

'I suppose not,' he had said, 'but I'd like to know why you want to.'

'We'll tell you later.'

The officers looked round the flat and soon became most interested in a bundle of £1 notes they discovered in a desk.

'D'you often keep money like this in the house?'

'No.'

'D'you mind telling us where you got these?'

Again William hesitated.

'A man gave them to me.'

'That was very nice of him. Would you tell us his name?'

'Thompson.'

'Where does he live?'

'I don't know.'

'Where did you last see him?'

'Here.'

'Where is he now?'

'I don't know.'

'How long have you known him?'

'Oh, for years. We were at school together.'

'What school?'

'I forget.'

'You forget?'

'I'm sorry. I made a mistake. We weren't at school together. I meant I'd known him since my schooldays.'

'An odd mistake to make. Where were you at school?'

'What does that matter?'

'It doesn't really. So you've known this man Thompson for years, and he gave you these notes. What else can you tell us about him?'

'Nothing, really.'

'That's strange. What does he do for a living?'

'I don't know.'

'Why did he give you these notes—£25 worth?'

'I don't really know.'

'You're sure there is a Mr Thompson?'

'Of course. My wife has seen him.'

'Is that correct, Mrs Burford?'

'Of course it is,' said Lesley. 'He's tall, and fair, with a straight nose.'

'So is your husband as a matter of fact,' the sergeant had said.

'Yes,' said Lesley, 'they are rather alike.'

'Extraordinary,' said the sergeant. 'You're quite sure that they're not so alike as to be one and the same person?'

'Of course not,' said Lesley indignantly.

'You've seen the two together, Mrs Burford, have you?'

'Certainly I have.'

'Well, that proves it, doesn't it, unless you were seeing double—or you're not telling us the truth.'

'Well, I wasn't seeing double and I am telling the truth.'

'How many pairs of trousers have you got?' was the next and unexpected question the sergeant had asked.

'What on earth d'you mean?'

'Just answer the question, please. How many?'

'Three. No, four.'

'It's five if you include an old pair of white flannels,'
said Lesley.

'May we see them?'

'If you really want to.'

'We do.'

William and Lesley brought out the four pairs of
trousers, and the police officers proceeded to turn down
the turn-ups of each and place a sample of the dust into
little boxes. They repeated the process with the pair he
was wearing.

'Which were you wearing when you went for that little
evening walk five days ago?'

'These.'

The officer made a special note on the label of the box
into which he had put the dust from those trousers.

'Mr Burford,' the sergeant had said, when they had
finished, 'I should like to take away these notes. I'll give
you a receipt for them, but I have reason to believe they
were stolen from the bank which was robbed five nights
ago. You may have read about it.'

William had gone white.

'You're not suggesting . . .?'

'I'm not suggesting anything at the moment, but I may
want to call back and see you again.'

That was the substance of the sergeant's evidence
relating to his first interview with William, and there was
no real dispute about it. Naturally the sergeant did not
state in evidence that he did not believe the story about
Mr Thompson. He was so used to such stories. William's
version was merely a slight variation of a well-known
theme, which runs as follows:

'Where did you get this?'—'this' being some article
which was known to have been stolen.

'From a man.'

'What's his name?'

'Fred.'

'What is his other name?'

'Dunno.'

'Where does he live?'

'Dunno.'

'Where did you meet him?'

'At the market.'

'Is that where you usually see him?'

'Yes.'

'Will he be there now?'

'Shouldn't think so.'

'Tomorrow, then?'

'He never goes Tuesdays.'

'Well, the day after—or the day after that. Tell us when you will be able to show him to us?'

'As a matter of fact I think he's left London. Talked of going abroad.'

William's story of Mr Thompson was not, in the sergeant's view, far removed from this classic model. The sergeant's story continued with his second interview with William and Lesley. On this occasion he was able to inform them that the notes had been positively identified —by cashiers' writing on them—as notes which had been taken in the bank robbery. And worse than that, from the Burfords' point of view, he also informed them that dust from William's trousers had been identified as precisely similar to dust from the bank's strong room. William was then asked to attend an identification parade, where he was identified by the first witness.

It was after this identification parade that William produced his alibi. He said that he was mistaken in saying that he had gone for a walk by himself. That was the night before. On the night of the bank robbery he was in bed with his wife and she could corroborate his story. William also now became rather more confiding about Mr Thompson and, after he had been charged with the robbery, he said that he had been to race-meetings with

him and that it was as a reward for his services during
those meetings that the money had been paid to him. He
had no idea that it was stolen.

Asked to account for the dust in his trousers, William
was unable to give any explanation.

'Your suggestion is,' the sergeant had said to him, 'that
this man Thompson must have been the thief. You didn't
lend your trousers to him I suppose?'

No, William had not.

So the case against William was a very strong one and
his last-minute alibi obviously shaky. Even a better judge
than Mr Justice Carstairs would have felt pretty certain
of his guilt. But a better judge would not have shown it.

CHAPTER FOUR

Verdict

EVENTUALLY the time came for William to give
evidence. He said that he had had nothing to do
with the robbery, and insisted that he was in bed
with his wife at the time. He had not seen Thompson
since before the war until he called on him a week or so
before the robbery. They went to a few race-meetings
together and he assisted Thompson by putting money on
horses for him. If they won, Thompson gave him a present.
That accounted for the £25, which had been given to him
the morning after the robbery when they had gone to a
race-meeting near London. They had come home from
the meeting and Lesley had given them a cup of tea. That
was the last he had seen of Thompson. It was just a
mistake when he said he had been at school with Thompson. He was upset by the police officers and made a slip.
As to the alibi, he had simply got the days wrong when he
was first asked to account for his movements. The policeman who identified him must be mistaken. The dust in
the trouser turn-ups was either a coincidence or Thompson
must have put it there.

'Thompson,' repeated counsel for the prosecution,
'Thompson is the villain of the piece, you say?'

'Yes,' said William.

'I gather that you agree that he looks something like
you?'

'I can't really say, but I agree my wife said so.'

'And she should know?'

'Presumably.'

'Now, Burford, you're an educated man. You were at a public school, weren't you?'

'Yes.'

'Which?'

'Must I say?'

'Of course you must say,' said the judge. 'No doubt they've produced some useful citizens in addition to yourself,' he added.

'Really, my Lord,' said Mr Empton, 'I must respectfully protest at that remark.'

'Indeed?' said the judge. 'Do you object to my classing your client along with others as a useful citizen? So he is, unless and until the jury decide otherwise,' and the judge gave the jury one of those looks. He was in fact rather overdoing it, a dangerous thing for a judge who wants a conviction. It sometimes so inflames an intelligent jury that they acquit, even somewhat perversely.

'Well,' went on prosecuting counsel, 'what was the school?'

'St James's.'

'A very excellent school, no doubt.'

'Naturally I think so.'

'Then why did you at first tell Sergeant Brown that you'd forgotten the name?'

'I was muddled.'

'But I don't understand,' said the judge. 'I suppose it's possible that by accident you said a man had been at school with you, when you really meant that you had known him since your schooldays, but personally I cannot for the life of me follow why you should say you'd forgotten the name of the school.'

'I didn't want to bring the name of the school into it.'

'You mean you thought it might bring disgrace on the school?'

'Well, I did not know . . . I didn't see what the school had got to do with it.'

'Well—you mean that, for one reason or another, you

B

didn't want to tell the police officer the name of your school—and so you said you'd forgotten it?'

'Yes.'

'Then why did you answer counsel a moment ago and say that the reason you said you'd forgotten the name of your own school was because you were muddled?'

'Did I say that?'

'You know you said it.'

'Well—I was muddled.'

'But that wasn't why you said you'd forgotten the name of your school?'

'I suppose not.'

'Then it was a lie?'

'I didn't mean to lie.'

'Then why say something that isn't true? It's very difficult for the jury, you know,' went on the judge, 'unless you pay some attention to the oath you took not so very long ago.'

'I'm sorry, my Lord.'

'There's no need to apologise. I was just warning you for your own good.'

The judge then invited prosecuting counsel to continue.

'So you were in bed with your wife when the missing Mr Thompson robbed the bank?'

'I suppose so.'

'You suppose so? I thought that was your case.'

'Well, I didn't see him rob the bank, did I?'

'Quite right, Burford, you didn't see him rob the bank. I'm obliged to you for the correction. You merely assumed, from his presenting you with the money and dust which came from the bank that he was the thief?'

'Yes.'

'And unfortunately the policeman identified you and not him.'

'You've already said we're alike.'

'No—it was your wife who said that. And I suppose that, if there were no Mr Thompson and it really was you all the time, it was quite a good idea for your wife to say that?'

'She said it because it was true.'

'So you say. But suppose it wasn't true—it would have been a sensible thing to say, wouldn't it?'

'I've never thought about it.'

'Well think about it,' said the judge. 'Everyone can make mistakes, can't they, but unless the police officer's evidence is a mistake, it's pretty damning, isn't it? So it makes it much easier to persuade someone—the jury, for example—that it is a mistake, if you and Mr Thompson are alike, doesn't it?'

'I suppose so.'

'And you had a good deal in common, hadn't you,' went on counsel, 'the money and the dust?'

William made no answer.

'And—for a moment or two anyway—until the mistake was discovered—the same school? No don't bother to answer.' And counsel for the prosecution sat down. There was no re-examination.

'Your next witness, Mr Empton, please,' said the judge.

'That is the case for the defence, my Lord.'

'No other witnesses?'

'No, my Lord.'

The judge sighed.

'Oh, very well,' he said. 'Do you propose to address the jury?' and he turned to counsel for the prosecution, plainly indicating that the case was so clear that no such address was necessary.

'Very shortly, my Lord,' said counsel, and, keeping his word, he made a five minute speech in which he effectively ridiculed William's alibi and referred tellingly to the undisputed facts of the case. Mr Empton then did the best he could in reply.

Empton's best point was that fingerprints had been found on the scene of the crime which were proved not to have been William's; but this was evidence of a very negative type. It was obvious that more than one man must have been involved in the affair and accordingly the fact that another man's prints and not William's were found was little help. But Mr Empton was grateful to have even this point to urge. He had wondered whether to suggest that the prints might have been those of Mr Thompson, but there was a feeling in the court—which he shared—that Mr Thompson did not exist. And so he left out this suggestion. He could not risk the smile which he felt the point might raise on the faces of some members of the jury.

When Mr Empton had finished his speech, the judge proceeded to sum up.

'Let me first of all say,' he began, 'that it is not for the accused to prove his innocence but for the prosecution to prove his guilt. And they must prove it beyond all reasonable doubt. Counsel for the prosecution submits that has been done. Mr Empton contends that it has not. It is for you, and you alone, to say which of them is right.'

The judge then went on to deal with the facts. Eventually he came to William's alibi.

'Or should I say alibis?' he said, 'for you will remember that it is common ground that at first the accused said he was walking alone in the streets. Later on he improved on that by saying he was with his wife. I say improved because two witnesses to an alibi are no doubt better than one. That is, they are better if you believe them. Of course, one witness whom you believe is better than fifty —or even two—whom you don't. But in fact you've only seen one witness for the defence. It is certainly a matter for you to decide but, if Mr Thompson really does exist, you might have thought that the prisoner's wife would have gone into the witness box to confirm it. We are told that she is in the precincts of the court. So the walk into the witness box should not have been too far for her. Why is she silent? You have heard counsel for the prosecution, in cross-examining the accused, pour scorn on this story of a Mr Thompson, this evanescent person, resembling in looks the accused and even in what he keeps in his trouser turn-ups. If you had been the wife of the prisoner, and had seen this Mr Thompson, could you have resisted the urge to add the weight of your word to that of your husband? She too was the other witness to the alibi. No, witness is the wrong word. She is said to have been with the prisoner when the crime was committed. She is said to have seen this Mr Thompson—but she is not a witness. What you have to ask yourselves, members of the jury, is why not? Why not?' The judge paused. In the middle of the pause there was a sensation.

'I want to give evidence, my Lord,' shouted Lesley from the gallery.

'Silence,' said the usher.

'One moment,' said the judge. 'Was that your client's wife, Mr Empton?' he asked.

'Yes, my Lord.'

'Did I understand that she now says she would like to give evidence?'

'Yes, my Lord.'

'D'you make any application for leave to call her?'

Mr Empton thought for a moment. He then decided that, having regard to the way the case had gone and was going, he had nothing to lose by applying.

'Yes,' he said, 'yes, my Lord, I do.'

'Can you satisfactorily explain why she was not called before?'

'No, my Lord,' said Mr Empton.

'You could have called her, but you decided not to?'

'That is correct, my Lord.'

'And now, in the middle of my summing up, you apply for leave to call her?'

'Yes, my Lord.'

'Your application is refused,' said the judge, and thought for a few moments. 'Let the prisoner's wife be accommodated with a seat in the well of the court,' he said. 'Where she would have been, had she given evidence,' he added.

There was a few minutes delay while Lesley was brought down from the gallery. When this was done the judge addressed her.

'Do you wish to remain in court during my summing up,' he asked her.

'Yes, my Lord, please.'

'Well, you must keep quiet then.'

'I want to speak for my husband.'

'You have had the chance and not taken it. It is too late.'

'But, my Lord . . .'

'Be quiet, madam. If you interrupt again I may have to deal with you for contempt of court.'

Lesley sat down and the judge continued his summing up.

'Members of the jury,' he said, 'no doubt you have wondered what has been happening in the last few minutes. And well you may. And let me tell you, so have I. I may also tell you that never since I came to the Bar, let alone became a judge, have I heard such a piece of gross impertinence offered to judge and jury in charge of a case. Here was a man who was afforded the entire rights of an accused person. He was defended by counsel. That counsel was briefed by a solicitor. The case took several days in front of a magistrate before the accused was committed for trial, and this is the second day on which you and I have heard it. During all that time the accused and his wife and their legal advisers have known perfectly well that Mrs Burford was or could be an important, even a vital witness for her husband. They have had an opportunity for weeks, not to say months, to make up their minds whether she was to be called as a witness. Even right up to Mr Empton's closing his case she could have been called. You remember—and but for this extraordinary incident I should not have reminded you—I

asked counsel for his next witness. I assumed, wrongly as
it turned out, that Mrs Burford would be called. When
Mr Empton said that the accused's evidence completed
the case for the defence, I actually went so far as to help
him—in so far as I properly could—in case he had
forgotten, by saying "No other witnesses?" It will be
within your recollection that Mr Empton said there was
no other witness to be called for the defence. And now—
now that in my duty as a judge I comment on the fact
that she was not called, the woman has the effrontery to
say that she wishes to be called, and counsel has the . . .
what shall I call it—I think temerity is the best word—
counsel has the temerity at this stage of the proceedings
to apply for leave to call her. You may not have been
surprised at my rejecting the application out of hand.
What shall we have next indeed? An application to call
such evidence after the jury's verdict perhaps? Would
that be much more outrageous? I will say no more about
it, except that you should not allow this matter to
prejudice you against the accused. He is to be tried on
the evidence alone, though, of course, in coming to your
conclusions, you are entitled to consider any lack of
evidence too.'

The judge then continued his summing up and, when
it was over, the jury retired. They discovered almost
immediately that they were all of the same view. They
would all have liked to acquit William because of the
judge's bias against him, but nevertheless, having sworn
to try the case according to the evidence, they did not see
how they could let him off.

'Perhaps we could add a rider,' suggested one of them.

'What sort of a rider?'

'Oh, by saying we'd have had less difficulty in coming
to our conclusion if he'd had a fairer trial, or something
of that sort.'

'He'd send us all to gaol.'

'Well, that wouldn't suit me,' said a housewife. 'My

husband's expecting me to cook his dinner. No, I'm sorry in a way for the young man but he shouldn't break into banks. I vote we just say that.'

So in the end the jury somewhat regretfully gave their verdict of guilty, but most of them found it difficult to stomach the judge's smile as he beamed at them and told them that he entirely agreed with the verdict. And one of them could not contain himself:

'My Lord,' he said, 'I nearly said "not guilty," because you were so unfair.'

'What did you say?' said the judge.

But the juryman did not reply. He had got it off his chest, and did not propose to do any more. Indeed, the anger he felt was swiftly being replaced by fear.

The judge spoke to the clerk, who went very red in the face as he replied.

'What is your name?' asked the judge of the juryman.

'Thomas Honeyman.'

'That was a most improper observation.'

Mr Honeyman said nothing.

'Mr Honeyman,' said the judge, 'I am addressing you.'

Mr Honeyman got up. 'Yes, my Lord,' he said.

'I said that your observation was most improper.'

'Yes, my Lord.'

'You agree?'

'Yes, my Lord.'

'Do you wish to express your regret?'

'Yes, my Lord, for having said it.'

There was a slight emphasis on the word 'said,' which implied that Mr Honeyman was not apologising for having thought it.

'Very well,' said the judge. 'I had considered sending you to prison for contempt of court, but in view of your apology I shall overlook the matter.'

'Thank you, my Lord,' said Mr Honeyman, and felt mightily relieved. He was a man of some moral courage but it is doubtful if he would have qualified for a monu-

ment at the Old Bailey, as did the twelve jurymen who
in 1670 refused to do as the judge wished, although they
were locked up without food or water for two nights.

The judge then turned his attention to the question of
sentence. A police officer referred to William's previous
conviction ten years before.

'What were the circumstances?' the judge asked.

'My Lord, I understand that the prisoner, who was then
only twenty-one years of age, went into the motor trade
and got mixed up with some highly undesirable characters.
He was eventually charged with conspiracy to steal and
receive motor cars. The ringleaders got heavy sentences
and the prisoner received six months. As far as is known,
since then he has gone straight until this offence.'

'Bad company again?'

'I expect so, my Lord.'

'Not Mr Thompson by any chance?' asked the judge,
smiling.

'I don't think so, my Lord,' said the officer with a grin.

William was finally asked if he had anything to say. All
he said was this:

'I may have behaved stupidly when the police called
on me, but I didn't do this thing. You think there isn't a
Thompson. Well, there is. I swear it. And he's the man.
Not me. That's all I have to say, my Lord.'

'William Burford,' said the judge, 'you have been
convicted on the clearest possible evidence of a very grave
crime indeed. Hardly a month passes without something
of this kind happening. None of the money has been
recovered with the exception of the £25 which was found
on you. I disregard your previous conviction, which was
of a different kind and which you appear to have lived
down. Whether you committed this crime as a result of
sudden temptation, or because you are a criminal at
heart, I know not. But it must be made known to all
persons who contemplate this sort of crime that the
punishment, if they are caught, must inevitably be severe.

It must be shown conclusively that it does not pay. What may be considered heavy sentences have been passed in recent years but they do not seem to have checked these outbreaks. In consequence the price must go up and in my view it ought to continue to go up until it is a sufficient deterrent. And I publicly warn any persons who may be minded to go in for the same kind of law-breaking that, if they come before me, even heavier sentences will be passed than that which I am about to pass on you. You will go to prison for ten years.'

William seemed stunned by the sentence and the warders ushered him away before he could fully appreciate its reality. Lesley, sitting in court, sat absolutely motionless, her lips tight together and her eyes staring in front of her. The solicitor had to touch her on the shoulder and to guide her out of the court. She saw the whole life which she and William had built up together spirited away. All she could think or see was 'Ten years—ten years.'

Mr Empton went back to his chambers in the Temple.

'We went down,' he told one of his friends. 'I shouldn't so much have minded that. I expected it. He was guilty all right. But Carstairs was a real so-and-so. Never gave us a run. But there was one good thing. One of the jurymen had a poke at him. You'll read about it. And he got away with it too. Stout fellow.'

Meanwhile Mr Justice Carstairs was walking home.

CHAPTER FIVE

Retrospect

IT was the most uncomfortable walk he had ever had.
Any judge might have been troubled by the juryman's
remark, but for one of Mr Justice Carstairs' tempera-
ment it was almost as stunning a blow as the sentence was
to William. It had only been by extreme self-control that
he had managed to appear outwardly calm in Court and
to pass sentence as though nothing had happened. Nor
was the severity of the sentence any result of the juryman's
remark. He would have passed that sentence in any event
and, severe though it was, it was difficult to say that it was
not justified in the prevailing circumstances. Criminals
must be taught that robbing banks does not pay and that
the enjoyment of the loot may be too far off in time to
make the risk of capture worth while.

But the judge was not at first worrying about William
or Lesley or what the conviction and sentence meant to
them. He was thinking about himself. At first he tried
dismissing the whole affair.

'Ridiculous!' he said to himself. 'It isn't true anyway.
I was as fair as the nature of the case allowed. I always
am. Anyway it was only one of them who said it. He must
have been mad or he wouldn't have dared to speak. I
suppose I should have sent him to prison. That shows how
fair I am. I didn't.'

This conversation satisfied him for about a minute.
Then the doubts began to recur.

'Unfair! It's absurd. I gave the man every chance. He
hadn't a hope anyway. Then not calling the wife! I

wonder if it was that which worried the chap? But what else could I have done? No one would have allowed the application at that stage.'

This satisfied him for another minute.

'I've always been particularly careful not only to be fair but to appear fair. And I was in this case. What was the man getting at? What had I done? Nothing. It was a plain case and the jury had to convict. Unfair! Ridiculous!'

And so it went on all the way home, and, by the time he reached home, he was already telling himself that— even if occasionally he had been unfair—it would have made no difference. Well, man's verdict showed it.

He took hours to go to sleep that night and, when at last he succeeded, he dreamed about it and the word 'unfair' kept coming into his dreams. In one dreamlet he found himself talking to himself.

'You weren't unfair,' he said. 'You were just yourself.'

That woke him up. What an appalling thing to say! He *wasn't* unfair. There were lots of judges much more unfair than he was. It was intolerable. He ought to have sent the juryman to prison and kept him there for months. That would have taught him to tell lies about a judge. Now he could go home to his family and tell all his friends and acquaintances:

'I told a judge he was unfair, and nothing happened to me.'

But he did apologise. Of course, I'd forgotten that. He withdrew and apologised. Well, did he actually withdraw? What were his actual words? 'I'm sorry I said it.' That was surely a withdrawal. It must have been. He didn't realise what he had said. He didn't mean it—that's why he withdrew it. But then there had been a slight emphasis on the word 'said.' 'I'm sorry I *said* it.' How easy it is to imagine an emphasis where there isn't one. I'm probably too sensitive. The man was withdrawing and apologising unreservedly. He was just overwrought. Perhaps he had

domestic or business worries. It must be very difficult to
be a juryman in such circumstances. Could I write and
ask him if he really meant it, and explain why? Don't be
absurd. Who ever heard of a judge writing to a juryman?
I must be mad even to have thought of it.

And then for a moment, as he was considering his own
unhappy position, he thought of the Burfords. Well,
they're much worse off than I am. They certainly are.
But it's not my fault. I had to give the sentence. And he
was certainly guilty. I wonder why she didn't give
evidence, and why she wanted to later? Of course it
might have been something to do with that idiot Empton.
I never have liked him. He's an oaf, if ever there was one.
He could never be a judge. What a ridiculous thought!
But why didn't she give evidence? She was an extraordinarily attractive-looking girl and might well have
made a good impression on the jury. But, all the same, no
one would have believed her. Anyway a wife counts for
nothing when supporting her husband. Most of them do
—even if they don't really like them. But what am I to do?
This is driving me mad. You can't go mad just like that.
There has to be something wrong with your brain to go
mad. There's nothing wrong with mine. But what am I
to do? What am I to do?

The judge had had such soliloquies on a minor scale
before, but he had never had anything like this. He
remembered judges who could be classed as opponents on
the Bench. He remembered having complained about
them himself. Perhaps he hadn't been entirely fair to
Burford. Perhaps he *had* run the case against him. Dammit,
he knew he had. He always did. He just couldn't help it.
When he saw a man was guilty, he had to get him convicted. But it wouldn't have made any difference. The
fairer the judge, the more certain the conviction. Why
was it he always had to run a case as he did? He didn't
mean to. He'd go on the Bench determined to be fairness
personified and, before he knew where he was, he was

making some sarcastic remark, quite unnecessarily, at the expense of one of the parties. Just like too talkative judges who, knowing their weakness, determine not to say a word unnecessarily during a case—and then never stop talking from the time they sit on the Bench.

But it wouldn't have made any difference, surely? Thompson didn't exist. If the man was with his wife, why didn't she come and say so? And that ridiculous statement about forgetting the name of his school. Yet why did a man who was happily married and in a decent job suddenly rob a bank? Suppose there had been a mistake? What a terrible thing to happen. Ten years! I couldn't bear ten days—but ten years! And for something you haven't done! But he had done it. Of course he had. But a man must be tried fairly. It isn't a trial at all if he isn't. 'I nearly said "not guilty" because you were so unfair.' That showed the juryman was satisfied of his guilt anyway. Or there'd have been a disagreement. But why did the prisoner protest his innocence at the end? And it certainly sounded genuine. But lots of them do that. No good appealing otherwise. A good actor, that's all. But he certainly wasn't much of an actor in the witness box. Ten years! And that girl without him all that time.

Well he gets a third off for good conduct. That means only six and three-quarters. That doesn't sound quite so bad as ten. If he'd only given him seven years he'd have only had four and three-quarters to do. Perhaps the Court of Criminal Appeal would knock something off. He didn't like appeals being allowed against anything he had done. But he began almost to hope so. But even then— nearly five years in prison. 'I nearly said "not guilty" because you were so unfair.'

The words continued to echo in his ears.

CHAPTER SIX

Interview with a Judge

A FEW days later Mr Empton was surprised to receive a note from the judge asking him to be kind enough to come to see him.

'I wonder what I've done now,' he said to a friend. 'I had a few dust-ups with him but they were all over, I thought.'

'Perhaps,' said his friend, 'he was so impressed with your performance that he wants to ask you if you'll take a pupil for a friend of his.'

'He's seen my performances often enough before,' said Mr Empton. 'Somehow I don't think it's that.'

Later that day he went to see the judge in his private room at the Law Courts.

'Oh, Empton, come in and sit down,' said the judge affably. 'Nice of you to come over.'

Empton sat down and waited.

'You must be pretty busy at the moment,' said the judge, after a pause.

There is a tradition in the Temple, observed by most of its inhabitants, that, if you have a lot of work, you make light of it, and, if you haven't, you put on a show of being grossly overburdened.

'Oh, it's not too bad,' said Empton. 'Just jogging along, you know.'

I wonder if he is going to ask me to take a pupil, he thought. That might well be the opening gambit.

'Good of you to take the time off to see me.'

'Not at all, Judge.'

There was another pause.

'Now, don't answer this question if you'd rather not,' said the judge eventually, 'but I have a special reason for asking it which you may find not unhelpful.'

The judge stopped. Mr Empton broke the uncomfortable silence with:

'Of course I'll answer it if I can, Judge.'

'It's nothing very alarming,' said the judge, trying to get the interview on to a less constrained level. 'I just wondered what you'd put in as your grounds for appeal against conviction in the Burford case.'

'He's not appealing against conviction, Judge, only sentence.'

'What on earth are you talking about?' said the judge sharply.

Mr Empton was so surprised at this sudden outburst that he waited for a moment or two before replying.

'He's not appealing against conviction, Judge.'

'He must be mad.'

'I've advised him it's hopeless.'

'*You've* advised him that? Then *you* must be mad.'

'Really, Judge, it *is* my business. He's got quite a chance of getting a year or two knocked off on sentence, but to my mind it's hopeless to appeal against conviction.'

'What have you to lose by appealing against both?'

'Time and money. If we only appeal against sentence the case will come on much sooner and he won't have an extra month or two in prison.'

'What's a month or two extra, compared with getting off altogether?'

'Nothing, I agree, Judge, if there were any chance of his getting off. But in my view there isn't.'

'You utterly amaze me,' said the judge. 'Now, let me tell you this. I sent for you because I thought that you might have been embarrassed to put in your best ground of appeal. I wanted to tell you not only that I didn't mind but that I should support it in my note to the Court of Criminal Appeal.'

'I'm sorry, Judge, but I couldn't think of any grounds.'

'You're still in time for appealing?'

'Yes, Judge, we've a couple of days more.'

'If I tell you two good grounds for appealing, will you put in an appeal?'

'Well, of course, Judge, I'd have to take the client's instructions, but, if I'm able to tell him what you say and that it comes from you, I don't suppose he'll want any more encouragement.'

'Well,' said the judge, 'if you must tell him, you must, but I should prefer you just to advise him to appeal after all—that's if I can convince you you've got good grounds.'

'I'll certainly do that if I can, Judge.'

'Good,' said the judge. 'Now I'll tell you your two grounds of appeal. I don't care which order you put them in. First—the judge rejected an application to call further evidence, without first properly considering it. In other words, he never exercised his discretion in refusing the application—he rejected it out of hand.'

'But really, Judge, with respect,' said Mr Empton, 'if I had the temerity to say that to the Court, I'd be blown out in two seconds, *and* they wouldn't be very nice about it.'

'I tell you,' said the judge, 'that I didn't exercise my discretion. I shall tell the Court the same. That's cast-iron, isn't it?'

Mr Empton thought for a few minutes.

'Well, Judge,' he said, 'it's very good of you to tell me this, and it certainly puts a new complexion on the matter. But I shouldn't like to say it was cast-iron.'

'My dear Empton, just think. Here was the wife, the only other witness to the alibi, the only other person who could say Thompson existed, and you applied for leave to call her to give evidence. Of course you were late in applying; or rather, you wouldn't have had to apply at

all if you'd called her before you'd closed your case. But
she was a very important witness and, before the case was
in the hands of the jury, you applied for leave to call her.
The judge ought at least to have considered your application. He didn't. He rejected it out of hand. Who can say
what the effect of that additional witness might not have
been on the jury?'

'Well, I am most grateful, Judge,' said Mr Empton,
'and I see how you put it. I'll put it to my client and I
expect he'll agree. I'll certainly advise him to. But you
said there was another ground.'

'Yes,' said the judge, 'there is. It's just this.'

He stopped, as though not quite certain whether to go
on, but in fact he had made up his mind that he would go
on and was only considering the form in which he should
put it. There is no greater protagonist of a religion than
a convert. And equally there was no doubt that when Mr
Justice Carstairs went into reverse he went backwards all
the way.

'The second ground,' he went on, 'is that the trial was
conducted unfairly by the judge from start to finish.'

'But really, Judge, I couldn't put that in.'

'Of course you can, if I support you.'

'But it was no different from any other trial I've had
before you.'

The judge smiled a little bitterly.

'I hope that by that remark,' he said, 'you do not intend
to be offensive.'

Mr Empton became confused.

'I'm sorry, Judge,' he said, 'I didn't mean for a moment
—I mean . . . I shouldn't have dreamed of . . .'

'All right, all right, I understand,' said the judge. 'Let's
forget the other trials. We're only concerned with this one.
You can rely on all my interruptions for one thing.'

'But you were entitled to intervene, Judge.'

'Look, Empton, d'you want to win this appeal or not?'

'Really, Judge,' said Mr Empton rather angrily, 'I

want to do the best I properly can for my client, but I'm not going to make a fool of myself in the Court of Criminal Appeal for nothing.'

'You won't make a fool of yourself. I tell you, my note to the Court will state that I have read your grounds of appeal and agree with them. Now, let me see, you can not only rely on my actual interruptions and the prejudicial remarks I made, the scorn I poured on your client's case, but you can refer to the way I looked at the jury.'

'There is a limit, Judge. I couldn't possibly do that.'

'Why not?'

'Well, for one thing, it's not in the shorthand note. How did you look at the jury, anyway? How am I to describe it?'

'There is a point there. Let me think. I must cast my mind back.'

He thought for about half-a-minute.

'You're quite right. It's extraordinarily difficult to describe it in words. I tell you what. I'll do it now and we'll see what we can make of it.'

By now Mr Empton was convinced that the judge was out of his mind, and he decided that he would humour him in every way.

'That's an excellent idea, Judge. Shall I be the jury?'

'Don't be silly. I want you to watch me. The jury are over there—by the window.'

'Very good, Judge.'

The judge turned towards the window, but, not being a particularly good actor, was not able to assume any particular expression.

'How's that?' he said.

'Jolly good, Judge,' said Mr Empton.

'How would you describe it?'

Mr Empton paused.

'It's not too easy is it, Judge?'

'Perhaps it would be better if I said something, to get into the part. Yes, I know. Something like this. Ah, yes—

Mr Thompson . . . you were speaking of Mr Thompson—
although I don't think we are going to have the privilege
of seeing him—if, indeed, anyone ever has had that
privilege.'

Inspired by these words the judge was able to give one
of his famous looks to the window.

'How's that?' he said.

'First class, Judge.'

'I'll tell you how to describe it. Take this down.'

Mr Empton took out a pencil and the judge gave him
a piece of paper.

'Ready?'

'Ready, Judge.'

'Right. "From time to time the judge looked at the
jury in a manner which plainly said to them that the
accused's story of Mr Thompson was not to be believed,
thereby usurping the jury's function." Got that?'

'Splendid, Judge. Yes. I've got that.'

'Well, if you go through the shorthand note you'll find
lots of examples of that sort of thing. Put them all in and
say at the end that it all adds up to an unfair trial.'

'All right, Judge, I'll do it,' said Mr Empton, 'and
perhaps I could add at the end what the juryman said.
That would lend weight to it.'

'What the juryman said has got nothing to do with it,'
said the judge with some asperity. 'It's I who am saying
it.'

'Yes, of course, Judge. I'll leave out the bit about the
juryman.'

'Put in what you like,' said the judge, 'but I should
have thought that, if a judge himself says that he's been
unfair, it doesn't matter in the least what a twopenny
halfpenny juryman thinks.'

'No, of course not, Judge. Well, I really am most
grateful.'

Mr Empton got up and turned to go. Just before he
left, he could not resist saying:

'What a pity you won't be able to lead me on the Appeal, Judge!'

'I hope you're taking this seriously, Empton,' said the judge. 'I meant every word I said.'

'Of course, Judge, thank you so much,' said Mr Empton hurriedly, and managed to get out of the door and down the judges' corridor and out into the Strand before he broke into laughter. Strangers seeing him walk across the road might well have thought him as mad as he believed the judge to be.

As soon as he got back to his chambers he burst into the room of the first available person and told him what had happened.

'It isn't really funny, because the poor old boy's as mad as a hatter, but oh—good Lord!—if you could have seen him. And heard him.'

After he'd repeated the extraordinary story to as many of his friends as he could find, Mr Empton became calmer. He now had to consider what was to be done about it. Suppose he made all the allegations suggested by the judge and his note did *not* support them? How could he rely upon the word of a man who was mad? And anyway, if he was mad, what possible weight could his note have? It was a difficult problem and he decided to consult another judge whom he knew quite well, and who would not be sitting in the Court of Criminal Appeal when the case came before it. The judge whom Mr Empton consulted agreed to see Mr Justice Carstairs without saying anything about the case, to ascertain if he appeared normal in other respects. He was able to report that he saw nothing out of the ordinary about him.

'I think you'll have to put in the appeal,' was the advice he gave. 'After all, it's your client you have to consider. If this gives him a chance of getting off, it's your duty to take it, isn't it?'

So, after a great deal of thought, and an interview with William and his solicitor, Mr Empton arranged for an appeal to be lodged against conviction as well as sentence. He worded the grounds of appeal as tactfully as possible, so that, if things went wrong, he would have a reasonable line of retreat.

Meanwhile, Mr Justice Carstairs prepared his note for the use of the Appeal Court, and anxiously looked in the list of Criminal Appeals to see when the case would be coming on for hearing. At last it came into the list and the night before it was heard was a very anxious one for the judge.

CHAPTER SEVEN

Court of Criminal Appeal

IT was obvious to Mr Empton after he had started to open William's appeal that the three judges had read Mr Justice Carstairs' note and were not a little embarrassed by it. Judges had been known to admit mistakes in the past (though not as often as they made them) but this admission of wholesale unfairness was quite unique. And it was particularly difficult for the Court, as the judge had done little more and little less than some of his colleagues of similar calibre did from time to time.

Mr Empton stated the facts and issues in the case, and then came to the first ground of appeal.

'My Lords,' he said, 'I approach this first ground with some hesitation, and wish to assure your Lordships that I should not have raised it in its present form were it not for the fact that I understand the learned Judge agrees with the way in which the case is put in my notice of appeal.'

'That is quite true, Mr Empton,' said the presiding judge, 'but the fact that the learned judge agrees with your submission that he did not purport to exercise his discretion on the question of calling the prisoner's wife is not conclusive of the matter.'

'But, my Lords,' contended Mr Empton, 'if he might have exercised his discretion either way, he might have exercised it in my client's favour, and, therefore, his failure to exercise his discretion at all surely amounts to a miscarriage of justice?'

'In certain cases that might be so, but I'm not at all sure that the learned judge in his report to this court does himself justice. He says that he never exercised his discretion at all, but dismissed the application out of hand. But was he really doing more than saying that it was a very bold application which no judge could possibly have acceded to?'

'For myself,' said Mr Justice Grain, 'I should have refused the application.'

'And so should I,' said Mr Justice Pantin. 'In my opinion no judge could have done otherwise. I don't agree with the learned judge that he never exercised his discretion. In my opinion he exercised it very quickly, that is all.'

'And with such an application,' said the presiding judge, 'it couldn't have taken any judge very long to make up his mind. Here you had the opportunity of calling the witness. No doubt for good and proper reasons you elected not to call her. Then, in the middle of the judge's summing up, just because he comments unfavourably on your failure to call Mrs Burford—as he was perfectly entitled—and I, for one, think almost bound to do—just because he makes those unfavourable comments, you ask to be allowed to change your mind. Really, Mr Empton, the proposition only has to be stated to show what the inevitable answer must be.'

In the face of these opinions, it was not long before Mr Empton had to proceed to his second ground of appeal.

'My Lords,' he said, 'again I should make it plain to your Lordships that I should not have raised this ground of appeal if the learned judge's note did not support it.'

'There's no need to apologise, Mr Empton,' said the presiding judge, 'furthermore, even if the learned judge's note had not supported your submission it would have been your right and duty to raise it if, in your considered view, the conduct of the trial had been unfair. Counsel must, of course, act with a due sense of responsibility and with due care but, subject to those qualifications, it must not be thought that there will be any animadversion on his conduct from this Court or, I venture to suggest, from any other Appeal Court, because he criticizes, however strongly, the conduct of the judge in the court below. Subject only to the qualifications I have mentioned, it is counsel's right and duty fearlessly to make such criticisms as he properly thinks are in the interests of his client. Fortunately, it is very rarely that the question arises.'

'I am much obliged to your Lordship,' said Mr Empton, 'but I repeat that in this case I should not have made these criticisms if not, in fact, invited to do so by the judge's note.'

'Well, let us see what they amount to,' said the presiding judge. 'First you complain that the judge intervened too often, and always contrary to your client's interests.'

'That is so, my Lord.'

'But a judge is entitled to intervene, is he not?'

'Of course, my Lord.'

'And, if there is a strong case against the accused, his interventions may sometimes—and even always—appear against the accused's interest?'

'Yes, my Lord.'

'Do you agree that there was a strong case against your client?'

'Yes, my Lord, there was.'

'Then personally I don't quite see what all this amounts to. Of course, a judge should not intervene too often, and he should never come down into the arena and join in the fight. But, subject to that and to the ordinary rules of evidence and procedure, every judge must try a case in his own way.'

'Justice must always appear to be done, my Lord.'

'Indeed, yes, Mr Empton. And does it not appear to have been done in this case? What other verdict could the jury have returned? Even the juryman who made that most improper observation, so leniently regarded by the learned judge, felt he was bound to convict the prisoner.'

'I see,' said Mr Justice Grain, 'that you even complain of the way the judge *looked* at the jury. Have you by any chance any complaint to make about the way I am looking at you now?'

'Of course not, my Lord.'

'It is new to me,' said Mr Justice Pantin, 'that a judge's face is to be a ground of appeal. I tremble to think how many appeals there might have been from my judgments on that ground.'

'It is not the face, my Lord, but the way he used it of which respectful complaint is made.'

'Well, how am I using mine now, Mr Empton?'

'My Lord, there is no jury to be influenced. That is the *gravamen* of the complaint, the effect on the jury.'

'Which do you prefer, an ugly judge or a good-looking one?'

'Either, my Lord, provided he doesn't use his ugliness or good looks unfairly to influence the jury.'

'And how can he do that?'

'Well, my Lord, there are various ways. By a wink, for example.'

'Are you suggesting that the learned judge in this case winked at the jury?'

'No, my Lord.'

'Then what did he do?'

'He looked at them in a manner which suggested that the accused was telling lies.'

'Are you sure you're not getting mixed up, Mr Empton? Was it not perhaps the accused himself who looked at the jury as though he were telling lies?'

'No, my Lord, it was the judge.'

'But apparently it was the accused as well. At any rate, that is what the jury showed they thought by their verdict.'

'I'm interested in this look,' said Mr Justice Grain. 'Can you help us at all about it by giving an imitation?'

'I'm not a very good actor I'm afraid, my Lord.'

'Try, Mr Empton. Suppose we were the jury. Show us how the judge looked at them.'

'I can't, my Lord.'

'But it's you who are making the complaint. Surely it's up to you to make your complaint good, or abandon it?'

'I've carried it as far as I can, my Lord,' said Mr Empton.

'I think you have,' said the presiding judge, who then proceeded to give judgment.

'We cannot help feeling,' he said, in the course of it, 'that the learned judge has, since the trial, been affected by quite unjustifiable doubts as to his own conduct of the case. For ourselves, we can see nothing in the criticisms which have been made. The case against the appellant was a very strong one and, on such occasions, it is inevitable that remarks of the judge may appear to be against him. We are not saying that every interruption by the judge was necessary or desirable, and it may perhaps be true that he did give a little too much the appearance of favouring the prosecution at the expense of the appellant. That appearance should, of course, be avoided, and, no doubt, the learned judge, if he considers that he made errors of judgment in his conduct of the trial, will, as we all do, profit from a realisation of those errors, but we see nothing in his conduct of the trial which amounts to a miscarriage of justice. The appellant was convicted because the jury felt sure of his guilt. So apparently did the judge and so do we. The appeal will be dismissed.'

The court then went on to consider the question of the sentence but in all the circumstances they decided that, although severe, it should not be reduced.

'Why did I listen to the old fool?' said Mr Empton on his return to chambers. 'All I've done for my wretched client is to get him an extra three months in prison.'

'There's a message for you from Mr Justice Carstairs,' said his clerk. 'He'd be grateful if you'd go and see him as soon as possible.'

CHAPTER EIGHT

At the Home Office

MR EMPTON went to see the judge but not very willingly. The appeal had gone off much as he expected, it had been against his better judgment to allow his client to appeal and he had been over-persuaded by the astonishing behaviour of the judge. But, while that was all very funny and made a good story among his friends, he was annoyed with himself for giving way, and he could not help thinking of his client who had not only paid for it but got an extra few months in prison as well. In consequence he was not particularly in a mood to humour the judge, however mad he might be.

'I'm absolutely amazed,' was the first thing he said, as Mr Empton came into the room. 'I wouldn't have believed it possible. Tell me exactly what happened.'

Mr Empton told him.

'I just don't understand it,' said the judge when he had heard the sad story. 'It's not your fault, of course. I'm sure you did all you could. It just shows what an unsatisfactory court it is. If civil appeals go to a higher court, so ought criminal appeals. There should be three extra Lords Justices to try them. However, we can't go into that now. We'll have to try to get this to the Lords. You can put in a formal application to the Attorney-General at once and we can formulate the precise grounds later.'

'The House of Lords, Judge? The Attorney-General's *fiat*?'

'Certainly. There's no time to be lost.'

'I'm extremely sorry, Judge. I have to sign the certificate that it's a proper case to go to the Lords, and I'm
very sorry, Judge, but I'm not prepared to do it.'

'Not even if I back you up and say that in my view it is
a case for the Lords?'

'I'm afraid not, Judge. You backed me up before the
Court of Criminal Appeal, but it didn't prevent my
making a blithering idiot of myself and my client getting
an extra few months.'

'But applying for the *fiat* won't add to his sentence.'

'I dare say not, Judge, but I'm afraid I'm not prepared
to take the responsibility of applying for it. In my view
there are no sufficient grounds.'

'I suppose you think your client guilty too?'

'I don't care whether he is or he isn't, Judge. I'm
responsible for giving the certificate and I'm not prepared
to give it.'

'Would you have any objection to my going to see your
client and suggesting that he should find other counsel who
would certify?'

'Judge, really!'

'Would you have any objection?'

'Yes, Judge, I would. I would have every objection. In
my view, for one thing, it's not fair to the man or his wife
to hold out more hope to them. The case is as dead as
mutton. The Attorney would certainly refuse his *fiat*, and,
if he went mad and granted it, the House of Lords would
dismiss the appeal and make some rude remarks about
the Attorney-General for granting a *fiat*. No, Judge, I'm
very sorry to have to talk like this, but I've done enough
in this case, quite enough—too much in fact.'

'I'm only trying to help, you know,' said the judge.

'I know, Judge. I'm sure you are. But quite frankly, if
you'll forgive my saying so, you're not succeeding.
Naturally I can't stop you approaching my client if you
think it's a proper thing to do, but in my opinion it'll do
no good to anyone. And, if you get anyone to sign a

certificate, it'll either be someone who doesn't understand
what he's doing, or someone with a reputation I shouldn't
care to have.'

'I'm afraid I've annoyed you, Empton. I'm sorry,' said
the judge, 'but I feel strongly about this case.'

'So do I,' said Mr Empton.

When he had gone, the judge decided that Mr Empton
was probably right. An appeal can only be made to the
House of Lords on a criminal matter if the Attorney-
General certifies that an exceptionally important point of
law is involved and that it is in the public interest that an
appeal should be brought. In a civil matter it is enough
to get leave from the Court of Appeal or from the House
of Lords itself, if either Court think that the justice of the
case makes a further appeal reasonable. No important
point of law need be involved. But, if the question is
whether you should be hanged or sent to prison for life,
only the Attorney-General can send you to the House of
Lords, and even he can't do so unless your case involves
an exceptionally important point of law. This looks almost
as though pure law is considered more important than
life and liberty.

Mr Justice Carstairs on further consideration had
difficulty in seeing how it could be fairly said that a point
of law of exceptional public importance arose. So he had
to abandon the idea of a further appeal. But he was not
beaten yet. He asked to see the Home Secretary and an
interview was arranged between the two of them. The
Permanent Secretary and the Chief Legal Adviser to the
Home Office also attended. Naturally, before doing so,
they had studied all the particulars of the case.

'How nice to see you, Judge,' said the Home Secretary.
'I don't know if you know Reynolds and Batey.'

They all shook hands and sat down.

The Home Secretary started the conversation.

'I do think it good of you, Judge,' he said, 'to have
taken so much trouble over this case. I wish Mr and Mrs

Burford could know. I don't think people always realise how much goes on behind the scenes.'

Having said that, the Home Secretary paused. He was not sure that his last sentence was a very sensible one. Nothing like this had ever gone on behind the scenes before.

'Thank you,' said the judge. 'Having ruined two people's lives I don't claim much credit for trying to put the matter right.'

'Oh, come, Judge, isn't that putting it a little high? I'm sorry for Mrs Burford, and all wives of criminals, but surely Burford ruined his own life when he broke into that bank?'

'Home Secretary,' said the judge, 'I don't believe he did.'

There was complete silence in the room after this bombshell. They could all believe that the judge had a bee in his bonnet about the way he'd conducted the case, but that he should now really think the man innocent had not been expected.

'But is there some more evidence we haven't heard of?' asked Batey, the legal adviser.

'I know of none,' said the judge.

And there was silence again. The Home Secretary broke it.

'Look, Judge,' he said, 'I'm only a poor layman. I read science, as a matter of fact. What am I doing at the Home Office? Well, that's another story. But I have to be guided by the lawyers in these matters. And I'm bound to tell you that everyone who's touched the case in the legal department, from Batey downwards—though, with his natural modesty I'm sure he'd prefer me to say upwards (and I must say he has some pretty bright legal chaps in his office)—everyone—all of them haven't the least doubt of this man's guilt.'

'They weren't at the trial,' said the judge.

'But the jury were.'

'Their verdict was my fault.'

'But you yourself appear, if I may say so, from your summing up and . . .'

'Yes, yes, I know,' said the judge. 'I certainly formed too hasty a view at the trial. I'm not saying there wasn't a strong case against the man. But that's no reason for a judge making a jury return his verdict.'

'But, Judge, I'm sure you're unfair to yourself there. All the members of the Court of Criminal Appeal said the same.'

'That's because I may be sitting on appeal on them one of these days. No, I don't really mean that, but I do think the system's a bad one. However, I haven't come to talk about that. The point is that I just have a feeling about this case. And I can't exactly tell you why. And I'll admit this—that if I hadn't been so grossly unfair, the possibility of the man's innocence would never have occurred to me. It was while I was considering my own shortcomings and the result of them—before I'd really considered the question of guilt or innocence—that I suddenly thought: just suppose he is innocent! And then I cast my mind back to the man in the witness box and in the dock. He was a bad witness I grant you. Personally I believe he was keeping something back but I can't rid myself of the feeling that, in spite of the facts against him, he's innocent.'

'You think Thompson exists?'

'I do.'

'Well, they may have been in it together. Has that occurred to you? There was at least one other person besides Burford involved.'

'Of course it's occurred to me, and of course he may be guilty. All I'm telling you is that I, the judge who tried the case, have a doubt about it; I have a feeling that a grave injustice may have been perpetrated and naturally, as I feel in large measure responsible for that injustice, I want it remedied. I want you to recommend a remission of sentence.'

'But Judge, how can I? Naturally I pay the greatest respect to anything said by you, and so do Batey and Reynolds and everyone else, but, if the Court of Criminal

Appeal didn't think your report sufficient to justify inter-
fering with conviction or sentence, how can I? I should be
usurping the prerogative of the Courts.'

'Yours is the prerogative of mercy. I cannot now ask
for justice. There is no means open to me. I tried to get
Empton to go to the Attorney-General for a *fiat*, but he
wouldn't. And I suppose he was right. So justice is out.
But mercy knows no bounds or rules. You only have to
make a recommendation and the thing's done. There are
no precedents in these matters. I, the trial judge, tell you
a mistake may have been made. That should surely be
enough to invoke the prerogative of mercy?'

'But, Judge,' said the Home Secretary, 'I'm sure you'd
be the first to understand that this prerogative of mercy,
although, as you say, it is available in every case, is not to
be lightly or capriciously used.'

'Capriciously!' said the judge. 'That's an odd word to
use when the trial judge asks for mercy.'

'It was a wrong word. I'm sorry, Judge. I apologise.
What I meant was that there must be some concrete
ground for exercising the prerogative. Some doubt, for
example, on the evidence as it stands. Some additional
evidence. Even evidence which was available to the
accused at the trial and which, therefore, couldn't be
called on appeal, can be considered by me. If there were
something you could say which would create a doubt, or
suggest that there might have been a miscarriage of
justice, I could consider that. But there must be something
that so far has not been considered, unless the case as it
stands itself raises doubts—and I gather you don't suggest
it does?'

'*I* have doubts.'

'Yes, Judge, but so might counsel for the defence or
prosecution, so might the clerk—so might anyone in
Court. Please don't think I'm equating you with them,
except in this sense that, if a consideration of the whole
of the evidence suggests no doubts, the mere fact that

C

someone at the trial—even the judge himself—has a doubt, is not enough. At least, so I am advised and, as I told you at the first, being a mere layman I must take advice.'

'You're not bound to act on it.'

'Certainly not, if I think it wrong. But I'm afraid in this case I don't.'

'You implied that a statement by Mrs Burford might affect your mind?'

The Home Secretary scented danger.

'I don't want to mislead you, Judge. If she could produce something concrete which showed that her husband might be innocent that would, of course, be most carefully considered. But the mere fact that she repeats her husband's story that they were in bed together at the time of the robbery, and that she says there is a Mr Thompson—those mere statements themselves wouldn't help very much. Of course, even they would be considered, but it wouldn't be right to suggest that her mere say-so would be likely to make me change my decision.'

'Then you've already decided?'

'There I am, a layman all over,' said the Home Secretary with a laugh. 'No wonder I need these wise men to guide me. No, of course I've made no decision. I was waiting for your help, and am most grateful to you for having given up so much of your valuable time.'

On his way back from the Home Office the judge spoke to Mr Empton on the telephone.

'Empton,' he said, 'I've just been to the Home Office to see if I could obtain any remission for your client. It might help if I could see his wife. Have you any objection?'

'No objection at all, Judge. It's very good of you. You can see the Queen and the Lord Chancellor and the Archbishop of Canterbury, if you like, as well, as far as I'm concerned,' he added, but only after he had replaced the receiver.

CHAPTER NINE

Unusual Conference

I<small>T</small> must be at any rate unusual for a judge who has
sentenced a man to seek an interview with his wife.
Even in the bad old days when there were corrupt
judges it is doubtful if a judge ever had a man hanged in
order that he might lay siege to his widow. The bad
example of David and Uriah the Hittite has, it is
believed, seldom been followed.

But, if Mr Justice Carstairs' motives had been improper
and corrupt—and they were certainly not—he could not
have chosen a more attractive young woman than Lesley
Burford. By nature she was in the best sense of the word
average. She was ordinarily intelligent, had the usual
likes and dislikes of a happily married young English-
woman. Anyone who has all these qualities to an average
degree is a pretty satisfactory person. It means that she
was very far from perfect. She was, for example, normally
truthful, but no more than that, and she would, if, in her
view, circumstances demanded it, lie as the average person
does lie. There is a substantial minority of persons who
tell lies to the Inland Revenue and cheerfully deceive the
Customs authorities, but (one hopes) they are a minority.
Lesley was not in that minority. She did not consider it
was necessary, or desirable, to cheat the Government or
public institutions. But she was not in the least prudish
about it. She just did not do that sort of thing. But, had it
been necessary to lie to save her husband, she would
certainly have done so and suffered no remorse in the
process, like most average wives.

Anyone seeing her in Court for the first time could

naturally not have been aware of her general character, but he could not have failed to be aware of her exceptional physical attractions. Mr Justice Carstairs had noticed them at the trial, but they had made no impact upon him, and accordingly it gave him quite a shock when he was introduced to her by William's solicitor, Mr Sinclair Hunt, in his office.

Mr Hunt was the best type of solicitor. He had one partner and two managing clerks and a practice which they could conveniently manage between them. He was careful but not absurdly cautious and was prepared to take a great deal of trouble himself over his cases. He never went to counsel for advice when he felt he was capable of finding the correct answers to a problem himself. In consequence, at his own risk, he saved his client time and money, for a solicitor who takes competent counsel's opinion is always protected against an action for negligence as a result of the opinion being wrong, whereas a solicitor who gives a wrong opinion himself, without going to counsel, is liable to be sued if his advice is wrong. The action will only be successful if the advice was given negligently, but it is a great temptation to a solicitor to avoid that risk where there is the least uncertainty about the answer to a legal problem, and quite often when there is not.

But Mr Hunt was a person of character and independence and he was able and prepared to form his own conclusions on matters of law. He was confident and inspired confidence in his clients. He had, too, a pleasant and comforting manner, and he combined an air of efficiency with sympathetic understanding.

Before the judge arrived at his office he had had a chat with Lesley.

'What do you think he wants?' she asked.

'I've no idea but it can only be to your advantage.'

'It wouldn't be trying to see if I was involved in the robbery too?'

'Good Heavens, no!'

'But he was so prejudiced against William, I'd believe anything of him.'

'My dear Mrs Burford, no judge would dream of doing a thing like that. I can guarantee that that is quite impossible. No judge would dream of playing the detective.'

'Well, I believe you,' said Lesley, 'but, if you hadn't said so, I'd have thought him capable of anything.'

'I can assure you that, if a judge once did such a thing, he would not remain a judge long. As far as I know, no High Court judge has ever been removed but he certainly would be for that. No, such a possibility is quite inconceivable. I've heard and said some harsh things about certain judges from time to time, but they'd no more think of going themselves to catch somebody out than of taking a bribe.'

'Well, what is it then?'

'Any suggestion I make can only be a guess. So why not wait till he comes and know for certain?'

'It'll help to make the time go. Tell me your guesses.'

'Well, for one thing, he may be sorry for you and want to see if he can help.'

'*Him* sorry for *me*? Never.'

'You can't be so sure. I quite agree he was a pig in court but that wasn't because he disliked you or your husband. It was just because he was convinced your husband was guilty. Such a judge might well be sorry for an attractive young wife. And don't forget, he saw you in Court. I'm not saying it's a likely thing but it is possible. Judges have been known to help the families of men who have been sent to prison, but usually it's done anonymously or at least by correspondence. Having seen you, however, and being a man after all, he may have wanted to have a look at you at closer quarters. It's most unlikely but it is just conceivable.'

'How beastly. I won't touch a penny of his money.'

'I told you I was only guessing. And anyway you mustn't be too hard on him. I can't pretend it is very meritorious in a would-be benefactor to want some return for his money, if it's only an interview with an attractive girl in the presence of her solicitor, but at least it's human.'

'Well, I don't want his help. What else can it be, d'you think, if it's not that?'

'Well, again, I'm only guessing. I suppose it is possible he's got second thoughts about the ten years.'

'D'you mean that?'

Lesley became quite excited.

'I'm sorry. I shouldn't ever have suggested it. I'm just using my imagination. Supposing he thought ten years was a bit hot he might want to make a representation to the Home Office, as the Court of Criminal Appeal hasn't done anything about it.'

'Then why come and see me?'

'To find out more about him. If I wanted to make a report about a man, I'd certainly think it a good idea to find out as much as I could from his wife.'

'If he should make a report would it do any good, d'you think?'

'On the whole I think it would. After all he's the judge who sentenced him.'

'How wonderful! How much will they take off?'

'Now you're jumping again. He may be coming for some completely different reason. Ah! there's the buzzer. It should be him. Good luck.'

A few minutes later their interview with the judge began.

'I know this is very unusual,' he said, 'and I need hardly say I spoke to Mr Empton before asking for this interview. I am very grateful to you both for seeing me.'

'Not at all, Sir Gerald. It's extremely good of you to come to my office. We would willingly have come to see you.'

'Thank you, but I think it's better here. Mr Hunt, do you mind if I ask Mrs Burford some questions?'

Lesley looked quickly at Mr Hunt. 'I told you so,' her glance said, 'he's come to pump me.'

'On what subject, Sir Gerald?'

'There's only one subject we're all interested in, as far as I am aware,' said the judge.

He had been so wrapped up in his own increasing desire to help the Burfords that it had not even occurred to him that there might be a hostile atmosphere at the meeting.

'Perhaps I should make it plain that my object is to help your client and nothing else.'

It was Mr Hunt's turn to look 'I told you so' at Lesley.

'I felt sure of that, Sir Gerald, but I do hope you'll understand my natural anxiety to protect my client.'

'Of course, Mr Hunt, very natural and very proper.'

The judge waited for a couple of moments before going on.

'Mr Hunt,' he said finally, 'can you advise your client to answer my first question, if she answers it at all, with absolute truthfulness. Her husband's trial is over, his appeal is dismissed. She can do him no harm by telling the truth. She may do him no good by doing so, but there is a chance, however faint, that, if she really tells the truth, I may be able to help. It is only a small chance, but without the truth I can do nothing.'

'I understand, Sir Gerald, and the question is?'

'Before you answer it, I should also say this. I had a feeling that your husband was keeping something back in his evidence. I may be quite wrong but I had that feeling.'

'You had a feeling,' said Lesley, 'that he was telling nothing but lies.'

'That's perfectly true,' said the judge. 'And you can now help me to know whether that feeling was right or wrong.'

'Sir Gerald,' said Mr Hunt, 'it occurs to me that the information you may be seeking is what has happened to the money or who were my client's confederates. That is the information that is usually asked of a convicted man in these circumstances. If that is what you are seeking, I can only say at once that my client absolutely denies that he had anything to do with the robbery. The only part of its proceeds he knows anything about is the £25 which was given to him by Thompson.'

'No,' said the judge. 'I was not going to ask about that. May I now ask the question?'

'Very well, Sir Gerald.'

'And will you advise Mrs Burford to tell me the complete truth?'

'May I have the question first, Sir Gerald, please?'

'You are suspicious,' said the judge, 'but I suppose you're quite right. The question is simply this: What is Mr Thompson's full name?'

No one said anything.

'Would you now advise Mrs Burford to tell me the whole truth, Mr Hunt?'

'Certainly,' said Mr Hunt. 'Mrs Burford, I advise you to answer that question truthfully.'

'And the whole truth, Mrs Burford.'

'You really think you can help, Sir Gerald?' asked Lesley.

'I can only say I want to do so.'

'Well his full name is . . . as a matter of fact he'd changed it.'

'Then it wasn't Thompson?'

'That's what he called himself.'

'Then that was his name,' said the judge. 'But what had he changed it from?'

'Wilson.'

'Wilson to Thompson. Why?'

'Why does any crook change his name?'

'Did you know he was a crook?'

'Not till William was arrested.'

'Why didn't your husband say that his name had once been Wilson?'

'I don't really know. I suppose because it didn't seem to make any difference what his name was if no one believed he existed.'

'Do you know what his full name was?'

Lesley hesitated for a moment.

'Forgive my asking,' said the judge, 'but are you hesitating because you're trying to remember or because you're not sure whether to tell me?'

'There's a third possibility, Sir Gerald,' said Lesley, 'I might be hesitating because I was making it up.'

'Well,' said the judge, 'do you mind telling me what was the reason?'

'As a matter of fact,' said Lesley, 'it was the first two. He had one rather odd name and I had to try to remember it, and secondly I wasn't sure whether to tell you anyway.'

'Why not?'

'Well, Sir Gerald, you can surely understand that, after the way you conducted the trial, it's difficult for me to follow why you should now be on my side.'

'Yes. I understand that,' said the judge, 'but I'm much more interested in the rather odd name. What were his Christian names?'

'Cedric Mattingly.'

'Cedric Mattingly Wilson? How d'you happen to know them?'

'Because he was at school—I mean because he'd known my husband since they were at school.'

'The same school?'

'No.'

'And it was Cedric Mattingly Wilson, later Thompson, who came to your house and gave your husband those twenty-five notes?'

'Yes.'

'And you would know him again?'

'Oh yes, certainly.'

'And it must have been he who put the dust in your husband's turn-ups?'

'Yes.'

'And at the time of the robbery you were in bed with your husband?'

Lesley hesitated before saying:

'Yes, I was.'

'Why did you hesitate?'

'Have I got to give a reason for the way I talk?'

'Of course not. But, if you are wise, you will.'

'There was no reason. I simply hesitated. I'm not used to being questioned like this.'

'And this man Thompson or Wilson looks rather like your husband?'

'Yes, he does. They're not doubles or anything like that. But my husband said that, when they were at—that, when they were boys together, people would comment on it.'

'Have you any idea how we can trace him?'

'The only place I can think of is a race-course.'

'He goes there a lot?'

'Yes.'

'I see.'

The judge got up.

'I think that is all I want from Mrs Burford, but I think I should like to see her husband. If I can arrange that with the Home Office, will you consent?'

Mr Hunt thought for a few moments.

'Subject to my client's consent, yes.'

'Do you wish to be present?'

'If my client wants me to be, but not otherwise.'

'Well, thank you both for seeing me,' said the judge and very soon afterwards he left.

That evening he sent a personal letter to the Home Secretary in which he stated what had taken place at the interview. He added:

'Having questioned Mrs Burford myself I am satisfied that this man Thompson, previously Cedric Mattingly Wilson, exists and I shall be obliged if you will arrange for the police records to be consulted to see if he is known to them. Although I still feel that I do not know the whole truth I am satisfied that further investigation of the matter is plainly necessary. I no longer think that this is a case where the prerogative of mercy should be invoked, but that it is one where serious efforts should be made to find the man Thompson. I shall be glad to hear that the police are prepared to take steps to try to find him. I am told that he is a frequenter of race-courses.'

He had a formal reply to this letter, and, a week later, was informed that neither Cedric Mattingly Wilson nor Cedric Mattingly Thompson had a prison record. There were, the letter added, a good number of Thompsons and Wilsons all with different Christian names. Nothing was said about trying to find the man. The judge waited a week and then wrote to ask what steps were being taken to try to trace him. He eventually received a reply that the police had taken such steps as were open to them but without result.

Angrily the judge sought and was given another interview with the Home Secretary.

'But, Judge, really,' said the Home Secretary, 'let us assume that the man does exist. There are only a limited number of police, you know, and if we employed the whole force on every race-course how would they find him? They could not question every man who answered his description, could they? And you must appreciate, Judge, that much as I should like to help you, crime is so prevalent at the moment that the police force, which is already inadequate, must be used for the prevention of crime and for the detection of unsolved crimes.'

'This one is unsolved in my view,' said the judge.

'But not in the jury's view, nor in that of the Court of Criminal Appeal, nor, I am afraid, Sir Gerald, in mine.'

'But at least something could be done. Have the police been on one race-course?'

'Certainly not, Sir Gerald. They wouldn't know who to look for.'

'They could take Mrs Burford with them.'

'Even then they could only go to one course at a time and I am afraid that in my view the time and manpower involved is not justified by the facts at present before me.'

The Home Secretary was getting a little tired of the persistent judge, and, though he remained polite, he took less pains to be conciliatory.

'I am sorry, Sir Gerald, I am afraid you will have to accept my decision that there is nothing further to be done. Unless, of course, some new evidence is forthcoming. Naturally that would be considered immediately.'

The judge left the Home Office and bought a newspaper. Ten minutes later he telephoned Mr Hunt.

'I would like to take your client's wife to the races tomorrow,' he said. 'Have you any objection?'

CHAPTER TEN

The Views of Brothers in Law

THE judge dined in the hall of his Inn that night. As he came into the room where they have sherry before dinner, he could tell at once that they had been talking about him.

'Go on,' he said, 'don't stop for me.'

Thus encouraged, one of the Benchers enquired:

'Tell us what it's all about, Gerald.'

'Certainly, if you're interested,' said the judge.

The Benchers of an Inn of Court consist of both judges and barristers, and constitute the cream of the profession.

There is probably no profession where there is a greater friendliness between its members. At all legal gatherings judges and barristers mix on terms of easy familiarity and between contemporaries Christian names are the order of the day. So when Benchers are together, views and confidences are exchanged with complete freedom. It was, therefore, an ideal opportunity to tackle the judge, if he was prepared to be tackled. But it is doubtful if anyone would have mentioned the subject if the judge had not pretty well invited it.

'Tell me just for my own amusement what is the wildest rumour about me.'

'They say you've threatened to resign unless this fellow what's-his-name is let out at once.'

'Well, I can put paid to that. I'm not such an ass.'

'What is the truth about the matter? That was an extraordinary report you made to the Court of Criminal Appeal. Criticising yourself for unfairness. Now, if you'd been criticising someone else, I could have understood it. But this is a sort of hari-kiri.'

'I suppose it is really,' said the judge, 'and, oddly enough, I didn't behave very differently from some judges I've known.'

'You can't have been as bad as Sammy,' said another judge.

'I don't know,' said Sammy. 'I think I'm rather fair. So long as they don't make me late for bridge in the evening I don't mind what they do. And, after all, I let those two fellows in the car case get away with it, and they were as drunk as lords.'

'Why?'

'A fellow feeling, I suppose. There but for the grace of God . . . No, as a matter of fact I summed up dead against them, but the jury let them go. Always do. Now, if the penalty for driving when drunk was an award of a couple of dozen Bollinger, a jury might convict a few of them. As it is, there's all this ridiculous business of being frightened if a policeman smells your breath after an accident. Every juryman who drives a car sees himself in the dock. A chap has to be senseless before they'll convict and even then they're just as likely to say he was ill as drunk.'

'Aren't we getting away from old Gerald's case? I want to hear about it from the horse himself,' put in a Bencher.

'Well, what do you want to know?' asked the judge.

'Everything. Tell us from the start.'

'Is she a pretty girl?'

'What made you take such a strong line?'

'Don't you really think he's guilty?'

'What did the Home Secretary say?'

'One at a time,' said the judge. 'Yes, she's a very pretty girl, and I'm taking her to the races tomorrow.'

'What!'

'Why?'

'Oh, you mustn't ask him that. It isn't a fair question.'

'Yes, you may,' said the judge. 'It's really a very simple

story. In my view, I made a so-and-so of trying the case and, having gone into it a bit further, I have strong doubts as to the justice of the matter. If he'd only got fifteen months or something, I'd probably have left it. But ten years is no laughing matter even with the remission. Now I believe there is a villain in the piece.'

'You?'

'Well . . . yes . . . me . . . but only in the second instance. The first villain got away with it but nobody believes he exists. I'm not a 100 per cent sure but I've got enough belief to want something done about it. Nobody will do a thing. So I've just got to.'

'But what on earth can you do?'

'Not much, but something. The wife says this fellow Thompson is a racegoer. Well, the least the police could have done is to go to the races with her once or twice and see if he shows up, but they won't even do that. So I'm going to.'

'Can I lend a hand?' said a voice. 'I'm quite prepared to take an attractive girl to the races once or twice. Might even pay for it myself.'

'If you're serious,' said the judge, 'I'd value your help. It may be quite a job doing it all myself.'

'But you aren't really going around to race-meetings with the wife of a convict?'

'Who's going to stop me?' said the judge.

The absolute seriousness of the judge suddenly got home to all of them.

'Really, Gerald,' said the Lord Chief Justice. 'Why don't you have two or three months' rest? You've been overdoing things and the case is preying on your mind.'

'The case is certainly preying on my mind, but I've not been overdoing things. And I'm perfectly sane. Or as sane as I ever am. Are any of us, when you come to think of that? We sit up there pontificating and making rude remarks and sending people to prison and how often do any of us look at ourselves and say "aren't you overdoing it a bit?" and I don't mean it in the sense you mean, either.'

'Don't be angry with us, Gerald.'

'I'm not in the least angry, I'm just explaining myself, as I thought you wanted me to. And coming from the general to the particular, suppose this chap is innocent—or, if you like, not so guilty—suppose there is a Thompson and suppose any of you believed that to be the case—will you tell me—any one of you—what on earth I could do, except what I am doing—or nothing? What would you do, Charles?'

'What would I do? To begin with, the problem would not have arisen. I'd have summed up fairly.'

'Never mind the summing up. Suppose there were a case in which you believed in a man's innocence and he'd been sent to prison for ten years and you'd done all you could along the usual lines and nobody would do anything about it, what would you do?'

'Well, if it's a serious question and you want a serious answer, I'd do what you've done up to the moment, report to the C.C.A. and, if that failed, I'd go to the Home Secretary. And if that failed, I'd mind my own business.'

'You mean you'd do nothing?'

'I shouldn't feel called on to do any more.'

'But wouldn't you want to?'

'I don't know whether I'd want to or not, as the situation has never arisen, but I know what I'd do—and that's nothing. It's not our job to do any more.'

'But suppose you felt strongly about it?'

'I feel strongly about a lot of things, capital and corporal punishment, drinking offences and so on, but I don't sit down and write to the papers about them, because it isn't my job. My job is to try cases and that is what I do. Indifferently, if you like.'

'Well, supposing you wanted to do something about it, what else could you do except what I propose to do?'

'I've no idea. All I can say is that, having exhausted the usual channels, I shouldn't do anything about it.'

'Look,' said another, 'I'm very fond of animals and I can't bear to see dogs straying in the street. It isn't fair to them or to motorists, but I can't stop every time I see a stray dog, can I?'

'No, of course not,' said the judge. 'But you can stop once in a while, or at any rate once in a lifetime, and that's just what I'm going to do.'

CHAPTER ELEVEN

Under Starter's Orders

THE judge decided to make at least one visit to the races before seeing William. For one thing he had never been to a race-meeting before and he wanted to see the sort of chance there would be of identifying Thompson, if he existed and appeared. He realised, of course, that the criticisms of his brethren and the doubts as to the propriety of his behaviour were probably fully justified, but a High Court Judge is answerable to no one for what he does, provided he does not infringe the law and provided, of course, his conduct is not so outrageous as to prompt Parliament to move the Sovereign for his removal. Such a removal has never taken place within known memory and the judge's contemplated behaviour was, at any rate, so far, not such as to make any reasonable person even dream of such a thing. He was simply going to a race-meeting, or maybe indeed several race-meetings to see if his companion could find and identify a particular man. If he were found, the whole matter would be handed over to the police. His behaviour was eccentric, was unwise for a man in his position, but there was nothing disgraceful about it.

He called for Lesley in his car and it did immediately occur to him, as they drove along to the race-course, that a High Court Judge at the wheel and next to him a most attractive girl, who was the wife of a man sent to prison by him, made an odd pair. So odd indeed that just for one moment he contemplated giving up the whole idea. But two things prevented him, first and foremost his real

desire personally to take at least some steps to make up
for his unfairness, and secondly his pride, which made it
difficult for him to run away from the battle in which he
had told his colleagues he was going to engage.

At first they hardly talked. Lesley said it was very good
of him to take so much trouble, and he said that that was
quite all right. That conversation lasted them for a
quarter of an hour. Then the judge decided to break the
ice.

'You'll have to tell me all about it, you know, I know
nothing about race-courses. I don't even know where to go
in.'

'I see,' said Lesley. 'Well, it all depends on which
enclosure you want to go into.'

'Enclosure?' said the judge 'sounds a bit like sheep.'

'It is,' said Lesley. 'That's what makes a favourite—
sheep.'

'I'm afraid you're talking in a foreign language, but
we needn't go into that now. Just tell me where among the
sheep we're most likely to find Mr Thompson.'

Lesley did not answer.

'Well, where? Which enclosure or whatever you call
it?'

'Sir Gerald,' said Lesley. 'I haven't told you the whole
truth.'

'That does not altogether surprise me,' said the judge.
'The sooner you do, the better for both of us.'

'D'you mind if I wait till we get there? Then we can
sit down quietly and I'll tell you. It's difficult while you're
driving.'

'Very well then. I hope you're not going to tell me that
there's no Mr Thompson?'

'Oh no! Really there is. I swear it.'

'I wonder why you didn't swear it at the trial.'

'I can tell you that now if you'd like to know.'

'I certainly would.'

'Well, I was going to give evidence, and then I had a

conference with Mr Empton and he decided not to call
me.'

'Why on earth not?'

'He said he didn't believe me.'

'He said he didn't believe you? That's impossible.'

'Well, he refused to call me.'

'But that's ridiculous. It's not for him to believe or
disbelieve you. That's for the jury. Of course there are
cases where it's too risky to call a witness, but this couldn't
have been one of them. I should never have thought that
Empton would do a thing like that. But perhaps I'm
judging him too fast. I'd better see what you've been
holding back from me. Perhaps that influenced him.'

'No, it wasn't that. He didn't know it as a matter of
fact.'

'Well, I don't understand it. Now tell me which
enclosure we should go to.'

'If you don't mind the extra expense, I think we should
go to the Members' Enclosure.'

'But I'm not a member. Are you?'

'No, that doesn't matter. You can become a member
for a day.'

'Whoever you are?'

'Well, you've got to look respectable and give your name
and address and so forth, and they like to have a look at
any ladies you may be bringing in, just in case, you know.'

They reached the race-course without any further conversation of importance and were soon lunching together.

'Now tell me,' said the judge, 'what have you been
holding back?'

'This man Thompson first came to see William a day
or two before the robbery. They hadn't seen each other
for a good many years and William was surprised to see
him. I ought to tell you that William, whom I love dearly
—more than anything in the world—is a weak character. That's how he got into trouble ten years ago. It
wasn't really his fault then at all. He thought he knew

everything at twenty-one and with a little capital left him by his mother went into the motor car business. He knew nothing about business at all and, when the much older people he was in business with assured him that what they were doing was perfectly in order, he fell for it. Of course, he shouldn't have but there it is, he did, and he paid terribly for it. When he came out it was difficult to get a decent job, but he really tried and tried hard, and he's started to make a decent career for himself. It meant an awful lot of work, and at the moment we have enough to live on carefully but no more. Well, this man Thompson asked William if he'd like to make a bit on the side. He said it was perfectly legal and, as far as I know, William's part in it was. But, when the police called, William became terrified that there was something crooked about it, so he was rather cagey about it at first. Then, when he knew of the bank robbery, he was worried whether the notes were part of the proceeds, and he became cagier still. You see, he knew the police knew of his record and that his previous conviction was for receiving goods knowing them to have been stolen. The same could have applied to the notes, couldn't it?'

'Only if he knew they were stolen.'

'Well, of course, he didn't until after the police came, but that, of course, gave him a guilty conscience even though he'd done nothing wrong.'

'You still haven't told me what he did for this man Thompson.'

'I'm coming to that. It was nothing really. He just bought winning Tote tickets for him.'

'You must explain. All I know is that there is a thing called a Totalisator and people can back horses through it. I suppose they're given a ticket and, if the horse wins, they get their money back and something extra.'

'That's right.'

'And I suppose when they've won, this ticket is a winning ticket.'

'That's it.'

'Well, I suppose everyone wants to buy winning tickets. I can see that. What's wrong with it? Suppose I bought a ticket and the horse won, I'd have bought a winning ticket.'

'Yes, but you'd have to name your horse before you bought your ticket.'

'Yes, of course, and that may be difficult. It depends how much you know on the subject, I suppose. But, if you choose the right horse, then you've got a winning ticket. I can't for the life of me see what's wrong with that. I suppose your husband knew something about horses.'

'No, he didn't really, but that isn't the point. The point is that he only bought winning tickets.'

'That was very clever of him. If everyone did it the Totalisator couldn't exist.'

'He didn't buy them from the Totalisator.'

'Do bookmakers sell them then?'

'No, they don't. You can back with them at Tote odds, but that's quite different. No, Thompson wanted William to buy winning tickets after a race was over from some of the people who held them.'

'Why on earth? But let me see if I understand. A race being over and a horse called Black Polly having won it and a man called Brown having bought a ticket from the Totalisator with that horse's name on it . . .'

Lesley interrupted.

'It doesn't have a name on the ticket—just the number.'

'Does that make any difference?'

'Not really, but I thought it better for you to understand as much as possible.'

'Very well then. Brown in other words having successfully backed Black Polly with the Totalisator, holds a winning ticket.'

'That's right.'

'And your husband was to buy that ticket? How much for? Do winners sell them at a discount? I can't see why, though. To save waiting in a queue or something?'

'Not at a discount. At a premium.'

'At a premium? You mean that, if Brown was owed £5 on his ticket by the Totalisator, your husband was to offer Brown, say five guineas, for his winning ticket?'

'That's exactly it.'

'But that's simply giving money away. I can't see anything wrong with it, but I can't see any object in it either, unless a man wanted to go bankrupt as quickly as possible. Or unless you wanted to do Brown a good turn. But then I expect there's some subtle point which I don't follow because of my ignorance of racing.'

'William didn't know what it was about at first but Thompson told him when he gave him the £25. It's got nothing to do with racing really.'

'I'm completely at sea. It seems a most unprofitable transaction but it seems only to do with racing.'

'It's to do with taxation.'

'Taxation?'

'Yes. As you know, there are a good many people who evade taxation one way or another.'

'Yes, indeed, too many, but I don't see how buying Totalisator tickets at a loss can help them in that.'

'Well, you will. Now, if I have a winning Tote Ticket, I can either cash it at the window or I can keep it and get cash or a cheque for it at the London office of the Tote.'

'Well?'

'Now, if you have a crooked business man who has had a lot of cash transactions in the way of his business and made a large profit, he can leave the transactions out of his books or fake them but he's got to do something with the cash. He could keep it under the bed or in a safe deposit but that isn't really satisfactory, because a lot of the things he may want to do with the money can only be paid for by cheque. So he has to bank the money. But, if the tax inspector comes to see his bank account, he's got to account for, say £2000, paid into the bank. If he just says, as some of them do, I won it at the races, there's only his word for it and the tax inspector and later the Commissioners of Inland Revenue may not accept his bare word. But, if he's had a cheque from a bookmaker or the Totalisator, that is pretty well conclusive proof that he did win the money at the races.'

'I'm beginning to see,' said the judge. 'What you're saying is this. If he were disbelieved about his £2000 he might have to pay taxes of anything from £1000 to £1800 on it according to his income for the year. But if he can prove it was won on a betting transaction he won't have to pay any tax at all. So, if the face value of the winning tickets is say £2000, it's worth his while to pay something more than that for the tickets, provided the extra is well below the tax he'd have to pay.'

'That's it.'

'So your Mr Thompson employs agents to buy the tickets at a loss and then resells them at an even bigger loss for the purchaser, but really making a profit for everyone. Brown gets more than he could from the Totalisator, Thompson gets the money he's spent and some more and the purchaser from him saves tens or hundreds or thousands of pounds in tax. The only people who lose are the public at large. Yes, it's a swindle all right. And anyone who took part in it knowingly would be guilty of criminal conspiracy. But you say your husband didn't know till the last time he saw Thompson.'

'I'm sure he didn't. But he was a bit worried about it. Like you, he couldn't see the point.'

'Why are you telling me all this now?'

'Well, you asked me how we could best find Thompson. And I had to explain to tell you. The only way of knowing whether a person has got a winning ticket in the Tote, except by chance, is to stand by the windows where they pay out after a race. You'll see a queue there. We want to follow anyone who goes up to one of the queue and persuades him to come out of it before he's cashed his ticket. Or Thompson might do it himself, of course.'

'Well, that certainly means we don't have to wander all over the race-course.'

'The obvious place to go is to the £1 and £5 pay-out windows. You'll understand that these tickets aren't worth buying unless they're for fairly large amounts. Occasionally, of course, there's a huge win for the holder of a ten-shilling or even four-shilling ticket, but obviously in the ordinary way only the higher price tickets are worth considering.'

The races began but neither Lesley nor the judge backed any horses. Lesley did ask the judge whether he wanted to try his luck, but he replied that he knew of more satisfactory ways of losing his money. As soon as winners started to assemble at the pay-out windows they went on duty together. Occasionally men came and spoke to a member of the queue but at no time did anything even faintly suspicious occur. Although the judge was able to sit down during and between the races he had to do a good deal of standing and by the time he had waited for the pay-out from six races he was very tired and that was the only result of his first day's racing.

CHAPTER TWELVE

They're Off

ALTHOUGH his first day's efforts were fruitless the judge had to admit to himself that he did not find Lesley's company at all unpleasant. He, in turn, set out to be as pleasant as he could be to her. He realised her great unhappiness and the strain of having a husband in prison, which he was, in a way, making worse. If nothing can be done to remedy a situation, an individual must accept it for better or worse. People vary as to how they accept an inevitable situation but the average person somehow adjusts himself or herself to it. But, as long as there is a chance that it may be remedied, hope creates a constant and telling strain on the person concerned and, if in the end, the hope, however slender, has to be finally abandoned, the last state is certainly worse than the first.

Recognising this, the judge made himself as amiable as he could to Lesley and actually took her out to dinner to make up for the disappointment of the first day's hunt. As the evening wore on, the natural awkwardness between the two began to vanish, and after a third glass of wine Lesley said:

'You know, you're not at all stuffy like one would expect a judge to be.'

'We are a bit different,' he said, 'when we don't have our wigs and gowns on. At least I hope so. Personally I think the uniform's an advantage. It gives us an appearance of complete impartiality. Though, now I come to think of it, I don't imagine that appearance lasted long for you. You must have thought I had a personal spite against your husband.'

'Well, you've shown me how wrong I was,' said Lesley. 'And, whatever happens, William will be thrilled to know that something is being done and that you're the person who's doing it.'

'Well, I'm glad,' said the judge, 'I've been able to convince you of my good intentions. I wish you could convince me that you'd told me everything.'

Lesley sipped her burgundy but said nothing.

'There was one thing I ought to tell you—but not yet, please. It might make you lose your belief in our case—and that I just couldn't bear. Will you accept my word that really and truly William is innocent and let me tell you this thing in my own time?'

Lesley then proceeded to take full advantage of the situation, which was that she had large eyes and an appealing mouth and that the judge had also had three glasses of burgundy as well as two glasses of sherry before dinner.

'I don't know,' he said, 'if you're a very wicked young woman. I certainly hope not. But, when you look at anyone like that, it's difficult to resist you. I imagine you can do anything with your husband.'

'I don't have to,' said Lesley. 'He always does what I want.'

'That's what I meant,' said the judge. 'I think,' he added, 'we should go and see him soon.'

'We?' she said. 'Can I come too?'

'I'm sure they'll let you in the circumstances. That's about the only thing they will do—let me get instructions from my client.'

At that stage in the evening the judge rather enjoyed referring to a man who had been sent to prison as the client of the judge who had sent him there.

'And I'm sure your presence will be necessary for my purposes.'

'Oh—thank you,' said Lesley. 'I can't tell you what it'll mean to me—to see him so soon. It's wonderful of you.

Don't take any notice. I'm going to cry a bit. No, I won't. There. I don't want to disgrace you.'

They talked about several subjects, nothing to do with the case—music, pictures, books and swimming. Lesley was an expert swimmer.

'You must look very attractive in the process,' said the judge, and suddenly realised that, as he looked at Lesley, he was putting her into a bathing dress, a red one with—but then he stopped himself. This really won't do. He quickly referred to the case again.

'What we must try to do,' he said, 'if we don't have any luck in tracing Thompson ourselves is to try to find some of the people to whom he has sold tickets and see if they can be persuaded to give some information about him. Your husband might be able to help us there. D'you think he can?'

'He might,' said Lesley. 'He never mentioned any names to me, but it's possible he knew some.'

'What I'm proposing to do,' said the judge, 'is to devote the whole of the long vacation, which starts next week, to your affairs.'

'You're awfully kind.'

'I suggest you don't get a job until the next legal term. There's nothing I can really do without your help, as you're the only person apart from your husband who knows what the fellow looks like. First though, tell me once again that he does exist.'

'He does exist,' said Lesley with every appearance of absolute sincerity.

On the following Saturday they went to the next race-meeting. They followed the same routine, except that on this occasion the judge risked ten shillings on a horse called Lord Justice. It lost. He had just seen the end of the race when a voice he knew called to him. He turned round to see a barrister whom he knew quite well but was not at all pleased to see in the circumstances.

'How are you, judge? Didn't know you patronised this

sort of entertainment. May I introduce my wife? Sir
Gerald Carstairs.'

There was nothing for it, and the judge had to introduce
Lesley. In mentioning her surname he can be excused for
using a trick which most judges employ when they don't
in fact know the name of someone appearing before them.
They make some odd noise which might be anything. In
this case what the judge said was something like this:

'How d'you do? May I introduce Mrs Borreforth.'

Borreforth is the nearest to the sound which letters can
give, but, as the word was half swallowed anyway, what
was certain was that it was quite unrecognisable.

'Haven't I seen your picture in the paper recently?'
said the barrister's wife, who had been famous all her life
for quite unwittingly making tactless remarks.

The judge hastily intervened.

'Now where did we meet last, Mrs Canterbury? It was
at the garden party, wasn't it?'

After a few minutes conversation they managed to
disengage themselves.

'I'm terribly sorry about that,' said Lesley. 'It must be
awkward for you going around with the wife of a bank
robber.'

'Never mind,' said the judge, and was about to add
something when they both saw a doubtful looking
character walk up to the £5 pay-out window and engage
one of the three people waiting for their winnings in a
whispered conversation. The winner remained in the
queue but the other man handed him something and then
spoke to the next man who waved him aside. The third
winner just ignored him. As soon as he had left the queue,
the judge and Lesley went up to the doubtful character.

'Excuse me,' said the judge, 'but do you buy winning
Tote tickets?'

The man scratched his head.

'You barmy?' he said and walked away. The judge
swiftly realised that, if you want to retain the dignity of

being on the High Court Bench, you can't talk to seedy looking individuals on race-courses.

Altogether they went to six race-meetings and drew a blank at each. The judge soon found it extremely tedious. The sport itself interested him not in the least, the standing about he found most tiring, he did not care to bet and, whenever he did, he lost, and generally he was quite unable to understand why such a large number of the population enjoyed a day at the races. It was expensive, it was boring, it was tiring and for the most part it put money into the pockets of some of the most undesirable looking people he had seen outside the dock. Bookmakers on a race-course, he thought, may be and I hope are good husbands and fathers, good rate-payers, good tax-payers and generally good citizens, but for a lot of loud-mouthed, dangerous or shifty-looking thugs they take a lot of beating.

It was while they were coming back from the last of these meetings that Lesley suddenly remembered that William had mentioned a name to her. It was an odd name and she couldn't think why she'd forgotten it, but, she said, she distinctly remembered her husband saying that one of Mr Thompson's customers was a Mr Hanamil Routang.

'There can only be one of those in the telephone book,' said the judge. 'I'll look him up.'

And there they found Routang, Hanamil, 8 Cloister House, W.1. Cloister House was an expensive block of flats in the West End. They decided that a call must be paid on Mr Routang. But who was to pay it, the judge or Lesley, or both together?

CHAPTER THIRTEEN

Mr Routang At Home

Hanamil Routang was a mid-European with some Scottish, Irish and English blood in him and not inappropriately he was naturalised British. He looked a little like a gorilla but was far more friendly on first acquaintance. He was obviously destined either for a long entry in *Who's Who*, including a statement of his many benefactions to national art galleries or for an imposing place in the Rogues' gallery at Scotland Yard, or possibly for both, the former presumably preceding the latter. He was at the moment at the one-yacht-three-mistresses stage but he had hopes of much better things, and he had several ladies in mind for whom he had take-over bids ready when he could afford it.

His purpose was to remain in England until he considered that the various individuals and enterprises he was in the process of milking were running dry. The extent of his success can be gauged by the fact that he actually paid large sums in income tax and surtax, though it should hardly be necessary to add that he evaded paying far larger sums. He looked forward to the time when it would not be necessary for him to reside in England within the meaning of the Tax Acts, but at the moment his activities were so continuous and concentrated that this was out of the question. It will therefore be appreciated that any means, lawful or otherwise, of avoiding payment of tax appealed strongly to Mr Routang, subject only to the proviso that there was no real chance of his being found out. He was prepared to risk imprisonment for a large-scale conspiracy to defraud. That was just a normal commercial risk. But to go to prison for defrauding the Revenue was a horrible thought which he would not even contemplate.

The problem before the judge and Lesley was not a simple one. It was unlikely that Mr Routang would give them any useful information unless he could see an advantage from giving it. Eventually they decided that the best course would be for Lesley to pay him an experimental call. It did not take the judge long to come to the conclusion that it would be impossible for him to make the call himself, and so, while Lesley was calling on him, he waited anxiously and rather impatiently in a near-by tea-shop.

Lesley had a piece of luck at the beginning, because Mr Routang happened to see her as she came to the front door, and, though he would not usually see strangers who came without an introduction, he was nearly always ready to interview attractive women, whatever their business. Even a travelling saleswoman would have a chance of a personal meeting with the great man if she were good—looking enough. So, within a few minutes of her ringing the bell, Lesley had been invited to come in.

'Sit down there, my dear young lady,' said Mr Routang. 'I know we can't have met before or I should have remembered it. What a charming hat, if I may say so. Cigarette?'

'No, thank you,' said Lesley. 'It's very good of you to see me.'

'It is a privilege. You seem to like that picture?'

Lesley had turned her eyes to avoid the intensity of Mr Routang's gaze and they happened to be opposite an Impressionist picture, though she was not really looking at it.

'Pissarro,' he said, 'but I won't tell you what I paid for it.'

'It's lovely,' said Lesley.

'It will be worth twice as much in two years,' he said.

'You're fond of pictures?' she asked.

'I'm fond of lots of things,' he said. 'The great day will be when I'm in a position to get them all.'

'Won't that be terribly dull? If you've got everything, there's nothing to look forward to.'

'Ah, my dear young lady, I only said when I'm in a position to get them all. There will always be something I want. How nice when I know I shall be able to get it. Window shopping I have never cared for. Would it be embarrassing to say that I was doing some at the moment?'

Lesley pretended not to understand.

'Window shopping?' she said.

'And I don't even know the name of the shop,' he said. A moment later he added:

'And by coincidence I don't even know your name.'

'Burford—*Mrs* Burford.'

'Ah—you have a husband. All the most charming women have husbands. But perhaps he is a long way away.'

'He is as a matter of fact.'

'Then,' said Mr Routang, 'let us drink to his return but not too soon.'

He got up and went to a cabinet.

'I have sherry at this time in the morning, but I know some people prefer champagne. Which can I offer you?'

Lesley accepted a glass of sherry.

'This is going to be a good day,' said Mr Routang. 'It has started so well.'

'I expect you wonder why I'm here.'

'Please don't tell me for a long time,' said Mr Routang. 'I shall be no party to accelerating your departure.'

They sipped their sherry.

'How charmingly you drink, if I may say so,' said Mr Routang. 'So few people notice these things. They look at a woman's legs and her face and how she walks, even

D

perhaps how she eats. But seldom how she drinks. There is a queer art in drinking. Personally, I love to watch people and animals drink. Horses, dogs, cats, sportsmen, manual workers—they all have their individual methods. But how few women know how to drink. If I might make only one small criticism, if I dare. It will not offend you?'

'Of course not,' said Lesley.

'The eyes,' said Mr Routang, 'should peer a little more over the glass. Only a little. Don't make it too obvious. Ah! that's perfect. You must forgive me. That's what I am —a perfectionist. I have, of course, never seen you eat. Do you perhaps happen to be free for lunch today?'

'I'm afraid not,' said Lesley and smiled slightly. She could not help thinking for a moment of the picture of the judge in the tea-shop, and wondering what he would do and feel, if she left him there and went out with Mr Routang. But she had no intention of annoying the judge. He was much too important to her. But Mr Routang was important too. She was even pleased at the blatant advances he was making. It certainly would not make her task more difficult.

'Perhaps some other day, or dinner perhaps?'

'You are very kind,' said Lesley, 'but I ought to tell you what I've come for.'

'Ah! now you disappoint me. With women business is always first. The weaker sex indeed! Those large seductive eyes conceal a mind which is intent on charter-parties or bills of lading instead of love.'

'What is a charter-party?' Said Lesley.

'You don't know? Good. Excellent. And a bill of lading, that means nothing to you?'

'Nothing at all.'

'Better and better. And love—that has some meaning?'

'Quite a lot,' said Lesley.

'Some more sherry?' suggested Mr Routang.

'Thank you,' said Lesley. 'Tell me if I've improved,' she added as she sipped her second glass.

This is too easy, thought Mr Routang. I wonder what she does want. She's not a detective, I suppose. Well, there's nothing she'll be able to get hold of at the moment. If she is from the police, I must say they've got good taste.

'Much improved,' said Mr Routang. 'I didn't think you could do better, but you must be a perfectionist, too. Well, I suppose,' he added regretfully, 'putting off the evil moment won't avert it altogether. Let's get it over and then we can chat.'

'I've got a friend who might be able to sell you something.'

'Sardines?' queried Mr Routang.

'No.'

'Silk stockings?'

'No.'

'Caviar perhaps?'

'No.'

'I give in. Not Indian hemp by any chance? I'm overstocked already.'

'Tote tickets.'

'Chicken feed,' said Mr Routang. 'How much?'

'How much could you do with?'

'I'm not really interested. How much have you got?'

'Could you tell me anyone who might take them?'

'You tell me how much you've got.'

'I haven't actually got any at the moment, but I can get them. That's why I want to know how much you want.'

'I never buy blind. I like to see what I'm getting.'

'But if you tell me what you want, you wouldn't be buying blind. I'd show you the ticket, the race-course and the result of the race.'

'How could I know who'd printed the ticket?'

'Then you could come with me to the Tote office and pay me when you'd got your cheque.'

'But how much can you do? A couple of thousand?'

'Two *thousand*?' replied Lesley.

'I told you I wasn't interested in chicken feed,' said Mr Routang. 'Suppose we compromise and have dinner tomorrow night.'

'All right,' said Lesley, 'I'd love it. Where shall we meet?'

'I'll send my car for you. Where shall he call?'

Lesley gave him her address.

'But don't bring any bills of lading or charter-parties with you,' said Mr Routang. 'We shan't have any time for them.'

CHAPTER FOURTEEN

A Capture

LESLEY described her interview to the judge in full. 'But what is the object of dining with him? That sort of man will tell you nothing.'

'I'm not so sure,' said Lesley. 'He's already pretty well admitted that he buys these tickets. I could threaten to report him to the Revenue if he didn't tell me.'

'That's blackmail,' said the judge.

'What's the punishment?' asked Lesley.

'Well,' said the judge, 'it's blackmail all right but it isn't actually an offence.'

'Well, that's all right,' said Lesley.

'It isn't all right at all. I can't be a party to that sort of thing.'

'You won't be. I will do it all myself.'

'No,' said the judge. 'I'm prepared to go on helping you but not if you use methods like those.'

'Well, there's no harm in my dining with him,' said Lesley.

'I hope not,' said the judge, 'but if it'll do no good, what's the point? I can't think your husband would be terribly pleased to know of it.'

'He'd know it was only to help him—just like my going out with you.'

'I'm not sure that I really care for the comparison,' said the judge, 'but, leaving that aside, I'm very much afraid that unless we get some information soon, I shall have to let things take their course. We've been trailing

round race-meetings without finding out anything. I'll go
to see your husband, as I promised, but unless we get
something to go on soon, I'm afraid we'll have to abandon
it as hopeless.'

Lesley kept her appointment with Mr Routang. She
was as friendly as she could be during dinner, and towards
the end of the evening she tried to persuade him
to give her at least one name to help them in their
search.

'Well,' said Mr Routang, 'I know one man I can put
you on to.'

'Oh—please,' said Lesley.

'I don't actually know his name—but I can tell you
pretty certainly how to find him.'

'That would be wonderful.'

'What should I get in return for the information?'

'I don't buy blind either,' said Lesley.

'Fair enough,' said Mr Routang, 'you can pay me on
receipt of the goods.'

'All right,' said Lesley. 'How do we find him?'

'It's quite simple really,' said Mr Routang. 'As you may
imagine, he spends a good deal of time on race-courses. If
you go round race-meetings you're bound to catch up
with him sooner or later. Well, there you are. You've got
the goods. Pay on delivery.'

'I've got a headache,' said Lesley, and wondered what
on earth she could tell the judge.

Although Mr Routang did not receive any reward for
his pains, he did not count the episode as a waste of time.
He considered that he was still attending the night-school
of experience. As in commercial dealings, so with women,
one must be able to tell at the outset whether an invest-
ment is likely to be profitable.

Lesley was glad to find the judge in a less despondent
frame of mind. He had worried throughout the night,
first that he'd undertaken the adventure at all, and then
that, although he had been angry with the Home Office

for doing nothing, so far he had only been successful in
proving how right they were, and in making a fool of
himself into the bargain. The laconic 'You barmy?' still
rankled a little. So he had decided that he would really
try to get some information out of William to set him on
the right track and, as there was a race-course on the way
to the prison, he thought they might as well have one
more attempt there.

While the judge was waiting for a few minutes by himself after the end of the second race, he noticed a man who
might have answered to Lesley's description of Mr
Thompson behaving in a rather peculiar manner and
standing near the Tote pay-out window. The judge kept
him under observation. Suddenly the man appeared to
realise that he was being looked at. He stared at the judge
for a moment and then made off hastily. As soon as Lesley
rejoined the judge, they tried to follow in the direction he
appeared to have taken but they could not at first see him.
They had gone towards the car park when suddenly they
noticed a small car with a solitary male driver drawing out
of the line of cars.

'Come on, quick,' said the judge. 'It might be a wild
goose chase but we'll follow him.'

They reached their car and were able to get started
before the man had got out of sight. They were soon in
pursuit. They both realised that the probability was that
there was nothing in it, but it was something to have a
definite object in view. It was, too, undoubtedly odd that
a racegoer should leave the course so early and apparently
only after he realised he was being looked at. Fortunately
the judge's car was faster than the man's, and though they
lost him from time to time, they were able to get his
number. They were unable to see the man's face and, as
he had crammed his hat over his head, it was difficult for
Lesley to form any impression of his identity.

'He's got to stop some time,' said the judge, 'and then
you'll be able to see him properly.'

But it did not prove to be as easy as that. After some hours they lost him and were beginning to despair of finding him again when to their delight they came across his car outside a hotel in a small town. They stopped and went in, but could not find him in any of the public rooms.

'Perhaps he's taken a room for the night,' suggested Lesley.

They enquired at the reception desk and were informed that a Mr Brown with the car number they had been following had taken room No 1.

'What do we do now?' said Lesley.

'You wait here,' said the judge.

He went to room No 1 and knocked.

'Who's there?' said a voice.

'Might I have a word with you?' asked the judge.

'Who are you?' said the voice.

'I'm a stranger,' said the judge, 'but I wonder if you could move your car for me?'

'I'm sorry,' said the man, 'I'm very tired and I've gone to bed. The car's not locked. Would you mind moving it? So sorry.'

The judge very gently tried the door. It was locked.

He went back to Lesley.

'Wait here,' he said, 'I'm going to get the police.'

'Is it him?' said Lesley excitedly.

'I've no idea,' said the judge, 'but I'm going to explain the situation to the police and ask them to send a man over.'

The judge went to the local police station and was back again within ten minutes with a constable.

'You will be very apologetic, won't you, officer,' said the judge, 'as there's probably nothing in it at all.'

'Of course, sir,' said the policeman.

The two men went to the door with Lesley a few yards behind them.

The policeman knocked.

'Who's there?' The voice was almost a whisper.

'It's a police officer.'

'What do you want?'

'Just a word with you, sir.'

'Wait a moment, please. I'm not dressed.'

'Don't bother to get up, sir,' said the policeman, 'I'll only keep you a moment.'

They heard noises in the room as though he were dressing. Suddenly they heard a window open. The policeman immediately tried the door. It was still locked.

'Open the door,' said the policeman in a much louder voice.

There was a noise at the window and then silence.

'Quick,' said the policeman. 'He's got out of the window.'

They rushed round to the back and saw a figure making hurriedly for a near-by wood in the gathering darkness.

'You leave this to me, sir,' said the policeman. 'He may be dangerous.' He started to run.

Lesley and the judge followed. By the time they reached the wood the judge was beaten and had to sit down. Lesley stayed with him. They could hear the policeman making his way through the wood.

'Stop!' they heard him shout.

A few minutes later a figure dashed past them, tripped and fell. The judge immediately sat on him, while Lesley called for the policeman. Fortunately for the judge the man must have been winded and did not struggle, and the policeman was on the scene before any more force was necessary.

'Now, what's the game?' said the policeman. 'Who are you, anyway?'

He turned the man over and shone the torch in his face.

Lesley gasped.

'Is it Thompson?' asked the judge excitedly.

For answer Lesley threw herself into the man's arms weeping.

'Bill darling,' she said, 'I didn't know. Please, officer, don't take him back at once.'

'Sorry, madam,' said the policeman. 'We've only just had news of the escape. Come along now, Burford. No nonsense now.'

CHAPTER FIFTEEN

Unusual Interview

T HE judge was given the opportunity of a chat with William at the police station, but William was not at first very communicative. He was very indignant with the judge.

'Not content with giving me ten years for a crime I didn't commit, you have to go and catch me when I escape.'

'It was quite unintentional,' said the judge. 'As a matter of fact we thought you might be Thompson.'

'What d'you want with him?'

'We're trying to help you as a matter of fact. Your wife thought that the most likely place to find him would be on a race-course.'

'Just what I went for,' said William. 'But why on earth do you want to help?'

'Because I do,' said the judge. 'Because I have some doubts of your guilt.'

'It's a bit late for that,' said William, 'but why don't you tell them that at the Home Office? They'd listen to you surely.'

'No,' said the judge, 'they won't. I've tried, tried hard. And so the only thing left was to try to find the man.'

'You didn't believe he existed.'

'No, I didn't.'

'Do you now?'

'Your wife assures me that he does.'

'So do I. But you didn't believe me before. Why now?'

'I can't tell you,' said the judge. 'To be quite candid,

I'm not really sure of anything. I think you and your wife are keeping something from me, but, in spite of that, I have a feeling that the man does exist.'

'Well, he does, that's certain. What d'you say we're concealing from you?'

'I don't know but your wife told me as much. And there's another thing. If this man exists, you were at school with him, weren't you?'

'No,' said William, 'I was not.'

'Both you and your wife made the same mistake, said that you were and then corrected it.'

'I can't help that,' said William. 'We were not at school together.'

There was silence for a moment and then William added:

'You will go on helping, won't you? Can you imagine what it's like being in prison for something you haven't done?'

'I can imagine few things more dreadful,' said the judge. 'It's because I think that's possible in your case that I've been trying to help.'

'For God's sake go on,' said William.

'Well, don't try to escape again,' said the judge. 'What do you think you can do by it?'

'I thought I might have spotted the man, that's why I was on the race-course. Then I saw you looking at me and I suddenly recognised who you were. I thought you'd recognised me.'

'Now is there any other information you can give me which can help? Your wife has told me of this fellow Routang but she's got nothing out of him. D'you know of anyone else who might have dealings with Thompson?'

'According to him,' said William, 'it's amazing the number of people who do. I don't know of course if he's telling the truth and he is the sort of chap who's pretty good at shooting a line, but he says he's got doctors, lawyers and even a judge on his list.'

'Nonsense,' said the judge. 'For one thing it's only of use to people who have cash transactions. And we don't.'

'Of course when he says a judge he might mean a justice of the peace. They're judges really too.'

'I shouldn't take much notice of what a man like that says anyway. But is there no other name you can give us or any place we might come across him? I confess I'm getting a little tired of frequenting race-courses, and the only time anything happened was today.'

'Don't I know it?' said William. 'But I do really want to thank you for all you're doing, sir. It is most kind.'

'You'd better keep your thanks until I've some tangible results,' said the judge. 'But don't escape again or we might catch you. And that would be such a disappointment for all of us.'

After a little further discussion the judge left William, and Lesley was allowed half an hour with him. Then William was put in a cell to await removal back to prison, while the judge and Lesley drove back to London, mostly in silence. Lesley was thinking of William and the judge was wondering whether he should tell Lesley that he was thinking of writing a letter to her. He had not made up his mind by the time he had reached her home. So the problem was solved for him and, as soon as he got home, he started to write.

CHAPTER SIXTEEN

To Write or Not to Write

'*Dear Mrs Burford*' (he wrote):

This is a difficult letter for me to write but after careful consideration I see no alternative. When I first undertook to help you to try to find some evidence that your husband was not guilty of the crime of which he was convicted, I must confess that I had little idea of what steps could usefully be taken in that direction. I have now spent some considerable time in taking the only steps which might be of help, with absolutely no result whatever. Nor, unfortunately, can I see what further steps can be taken. You would not, I know, expect me to attend every race-meeting in England (and Scotland, too, for that matter, for I have learned that racing takes place even there) but, even if I were to agree to do so, it might still be of no avail because I have also learned that on some days as many as five race-meetings may take place in different parts of the country. Although I understand that some jockeys hire aeroplanes to take them from one meeting to another on the same day, I should not feel justified in incurring this heavy expense, and, even if I were prepared to do so, it would still mean that on some days there would be meetings which we could not attend. If there were other steps by which I could usefully (and properly) help you I should be prepared to consider taking them, but, unless you are able to suggest any such steps to me, I am afraid that there is nothing further that I can do.

I am sorry to have to write like this, particularly just after the recent shock you must have had in seeing your husband recaptured, but I feel that it is better to say so now than to go on dragging out the matter interminably.

If at any time you receive information which you think may be helpful to your husband's cause I shall be pleased to consider it.
Yours sincerely,
Gerald Carstairs.'

Having written the letter he went to bed, but he had a bad night worrying about the matter. He had quite a vivid imagination and he pictured Lesley seeing the post and the letter in a handwriting she did not know. With feminine intuition she might guess who it was from and even what was in it. He could see her opening the letter with apprehension and reading it with something like despair. It must have seemed like a miracle to her to find that the judge who had presided at her husband's trial was on her side and wanted to help. As long as he was doing so, she could feel some hope that the nightmare would come to an end. But if he stopped what was there left? You can't expect two miracles.

And then he looked at the other side of the picture. Suppose her husband really were guilty and there were no Mr Thompson, then she was just playing with him, either in the hope that something might turn up, which, coupled with the backing of a judge, would lead to her husband's wrongful release, or just out of revenge or for amusement. After all, everyone but he had no doubt about the matter. The jury clearly had no doubts. Empton thought their verdict was right and that an appeal was ridiculous. The Court of Criminal Appeal had no doubt when they dismissed the appeal. The Home Secretary and his advisers made their view of the matter abundantly clear. Why on earth should he alone be right? Moreover, even he felt that the Burfords were concealing something. Why shouldn't that fact be the simple one that Mr Thompson did not exist and that Burford was as guilty as everyone else felt. He was a fool even to have contemplated helping the couple.

And then he thought of the few famous miscarriages of

justice which had taken place in this country, one even
quite recently, when a man had actually been wrongly
identified by a policeman. It was eventually proved
conclusively that the convicted man was not guilty, but
the jury had returned their verdict against him in a
quarter of an hour. They had laughed at his defence of an
alibi. Yet that man was proved to have been innocent of
that particular crime. Such occurrences were fortunately
very rare but they did happen. Was this one of them? If
it was, how appalling for the young couple. No amount
of compensation could put matters right for them. If Mrs
Burford remained faithful to her husband till he was
released in seven years' time she would be wasting all
those years of her life when she might be having children.
If she committed adultery and Burford divorced her, a
happy home would have been broken up.

A judge should be able to see both points of view, but he
should also be able to make up his mind between them.
This judge was quite unable to do so. He lay in bed
alternately satisfying himself of William's guilt and
convincing himself of his innocence, assuring himself that
there was nothing more he could do and then that it was
not fair to take on a job like this and drop it in the middle.

In the middle? Was it in the middle? Wasn't it the end?
Hadn't he done all he could do? There was certainly no
end to these conflicting thoughts. He got up and took two
sleeping tablets.

CHAPTER SEVENTEEN

On Holiday

WHEN he awoke, he got up at once and read the letter he had written, thought about it and tore it up. Then he decided to say it on the telephone instead. He picked up the telephone and then put it down again because he couldn't think how to begin. He was still undecided when Lesley telephoned.

'I've had an idea,' she said. 'Why shouldn't I advertise for someone who could give information of Thompson's whereabouts?'

'There's no reason why you shouldn't,' said the judge, 'but you must be prepared to draw another blank.'

'Of course,' said Lesley, 'but I thought it might be worth trying.'

Four days later she informed the judge that a man had answered the advertisement.

'He's a pretty unsavoury specimen,' she said, 'but he claims to know Thompson and says he's sure he can find him for me.'

'Well, that's good,' said the judge. 'There's no harm in following up any of his suggestions. But the way you speak makes me think there's a snag in it. Is there?'

'Not really,' said Lesley. 'It's just this, that . . . Well, I find this awfully embarrassing—you've been so terribly kind and I must have cost you quite a lot of money so far and . . .'

'How much does this man want?' said the judge.

'Twenty-five pounds, to begin with,' said Lesley.

'What do you get for the twenty-five pounds? What does "to begin with" mean?'

'Twenty-five pounds is for the first try. If it comes off, that'll be that. If it doesn't, he'll want more.'

'Well, you say the man's unsavoury; if he's a crook he could run up a whole lot of twenty-five pounds.'

'I know,' said Lesley. 'One's pretty well in his hands, but I thought . . .'

'All right,' said the judge. 'I'll stand for the first lot.'

'You are good,' said Lesley.

'Probably only foolish,' said the judge.

But in fact he was quite pleased to be able to do this. It solved his problem for the moment. He could easily afford the money, and providing it was a useful compromise between giving the whole thing up and doing futile things himself. So for a day or two he ceased to worry so much about the matter. After all, he was doing all he had been asked to do. For peace of mind it was cheap at the price.

One evening a few days later he received a very odd call from Lesley. He could recognise her voice but she was speaking very softly and in an extremely strange manner, so strange indeed that he wondered if she could have been drunk. She had always treated him up to that moment as he would have expected. She either called him 'Sir Gerald' or nothing at all and, though they had become on terms of easy familiarity, she had never taken advantage of that fact. Accordingly he was astonished to hear her say when he answered the telephone:

'Is that you, Gerald?'

He felt pretty certain who it was but none the less he asked:

'Who is it?'

'Lesley, of course,' she answered. 'Look, Gerald, do come down and join us at the Bear at Esher for dinner.'

'I beg your pardon?' he said.

'It's just on the spur of the moment, but I do want you

to come. I *want you to come terribly*. The party will be
nothing if you don't.'

It was quite plain that she was putting something into
her words which for some reason she was unable or
unwilling to say. For once the judge made a swift decision.

'All right,' he said, 'I'll come at once. I should love
it.'

'How sweet of you,' she said. 'Do be quick or we shall
have drunk all the champagne.'

So the judge got out his car and was soon on the way to
Esher. He was there within three quarters of an hour. He
found Lesley in front of the hotel to meet him. He parked
the car and got out.

'What is it?' he said.

'I'm terribly sorry,' she said, 'it's a washout, but I
couldn't think of anything else to do.'

'For heaven's sake explain yourself,' he said.

'He was here,' she said. 'Only left twenty minutes ago.
I just didn't know what to do.'

'Who was here and what did that extraordinary call
mean?'

'It was like this. My man was right and I found Thompson at Sandown. I couldn't let him see me or he'd have
bolted. I came by coach and couldn't have followed him.
After the races he came here. I could just get in and out
of the 'phone box without his seeing me, but he could hear
every word I said. I don't mean that he was necessarily
listening, but he could have heard if he wanted to. If he'd
heard anyone ringing the police he'd have been off and
away at once. And if he'd heard me speaking to you
properly, as I should have done, calling you Sir Gerald
and asking you to come quickly, he might have smelled a
rat. So I thought you'd understand if I spoke to you as I
did. I do hope you didn't mind.'

'No, of course, I didn't mind that,' said the judge, 'but
the net result is that I might just as well have stayed at
home.'

'I'm afraid so,' said Lesley, 'but I couldn't tell, could I?
And it was such a chance.'

'Well, next time get on to the police at once,' said the
judge.

'Well, of course,' said Lesley, 'I would have this time,
but you do see how I was placed.'

'I suppose so,' said the judge. 'And, now, I imagine your
doubtful friend will want another twenty-five pounds.'

'I'm afraid he will.'

'And, as a matter of fact, you ought to have someone
else with you and a car on these occasions. You'd better
get hold of a private detective. You really did see this man
Thompson today—really and truly?'

'Really and truly,' said Lesley.

'No doubt of any kind? No possibility of mistake?'

'None whatever.'

'All right. I'll pay for the detective. I think perhaps I'd
better arrange for one myself. I'll let you know who it is.'

So Mr Maclachlan of Hounds Ltd., private enquiry
agents, had the privilege of having a High Court Judge
sitting in his office. After having appeared himself on
innumerable occasions in the witness box before High
Court Judges it was a novel and pleasant experience. Mr
Maclachlan had in the past been told by different judges
that they believed every word he said and also that they
believed nothing that he said; that he was an admirable
witness 'as different from the normal enquiry agent as it
would be possible to imagine', and that his evidence was
'almost a classic example of evidence which had long been
recognised by the Courts as being of the most unsatisfactory nature.' Judges had said to him 'So you expect me
to believe that, do you?' and 'Thank you very much, Mr
Maclachlan.'

Hounds Ltd., which was in effect Mr Maclachlan's
other name, had a considerable practice and a reputation
for getting things done. Praise and blame came alike to
Mr Maclachlan. So long as it was one thing or the other,

he felt that his firm had pulled its weight. What he would have considered a danger sign would have been if his evidence or that of his employees had simply been ignored. As long as it was described as 'obviously truthful' or stigmatised as 'near-perjury' he was perfectly satisfied.

The judge explained to Mr Maclachlan what he required. He was to supply an agent to go with Mrs Burford and act under her instructions at any time of the day or night in order to ascertain the existence of a Mr Thompson, formerly Cedric Mattingly Wilson. As soon as he could be definitely identified the agent was to communicate with the police. The judge would finance the transaction up to an extent of a sum not to exceed £100, including expenses.

'That raises a point, my Lord,' said Mr Maclachlan, who, not being sure how to address a High Court Judge out of Court, was taking no chances. 'Suppose my employee was in the middle of tracking Mr Thompson when the £100 ran out?'

'You must use reasonable discretion, of course,' said the judge. 'Naturally, in the circumstances, I would pay any reasonable additional charges.'

'Thank you, my Lord,' said Mr Maclachlan. 'With my experience of the Courts I think it as well to clear up these little points before we start.'

'I quite agree,' said the judge. 'Now is there anything you're not clear about?'

'I think not,' said Mr Maclachlan, 'but, if I may have your telephone number, perhaps I may be allowed to telephone you, if necessary.'

The judge told Lesley to call on Hounds Ltd., and make the necessary arrangements so that she could be supplied with an agent at short notice. He then went on holiday in a happier frame of mind, but he gave Lesley his telephone number in case she needed him.

For the first couple of days at his hotel the judge was much happier. Since he had lost his wife many years previously he enjoyed holidays on his own. Oddly enough he liked his own company, though it is perhaps not really so odd, when one considers that, if you are a worrier by nature, it is much easier to worry when you are by yourself. The judge used to choose a comfortable hotel and spend part of his time reading, part talking to his fellow guests and part listening to some of them complaining how uncomfortable the comfortable hotel was.

He found, for example, Mr and Mrs Sugden-Placey quite a tonic, though, after listening to them for a week abusing each other and everything else in the hotel, he became rather sorry for them in a way. The husband was an indifferent shot, and an unkind guest, who had seen his performances on the moors and in the hotel, put forward the opinion that Sugden-Placey only hit a bird if he imagined that it was his wife who had risen. Then he let fly with both barrels and scored with each, but on the same bird.

There was usually some entertainment at meal times.

'Now I don't want to make a point of this,' Sugden-Placey would begin.

'Well, don't then,' said his wife.

'I haven't started yet.'

'I said "don't".'

'It's too bad they always put the toast on the table before we come down. I like mine fresh. If I've mentioned it once, I've mentioned it a hundred times. It's not as though we were only here overnight. We're here for a month.'

'You should come down earlier,' said his wife.

Little realising that he played very much the same game with himself, the judge took an unkind pleasure in listening to their bickering. He also observed how the staff, while maintaining an almost exaggerated air of politeness, saw to it that they were usually served last and that, if any inconveniences had to be suffered, it should be the Sugden-Placeys who suffered them. The simple moral, unintelligible to Sugden-Placey, is that, the less you complain, the less you have to. If, as soon as you arrive, there's something wrong with the door of your lock-up garage, your luggage isn't taken off the car quickly enough, the girl in the office is on the telephone and doesn't attend to you at once, your room isn't as large as you thought it was going to be and faces the wrong direction and there are no face towels then, if you howl at the top of your voice about every one of these disasters, you can he pretty sure that they will be followed by many more. It is not very easy to find a good hotel but it is almost certain that the Sugden-Placeys will never find one.

Such people are, however, useful members of society if, for no other reason, than that they give the other guests something to talk about. The judge never criticised other guests but he listened cheerfully to them criticising each other. He was quite a popular figure in the bar of the hotel. High Court Judges usually are. One reason is probably the fascination of evil. It is a great thrill for most people to see a man in the dock. The more serious the crime, the greater the thrill. And, if you have the luck to see a man charged with capital murder, and have a good imagination, you can picture to yourself what is going to happen to the unfortunate prisoner, if convicted. But few people get this opportunity. So it is a good substitute to meet a judge whose duty it is to pass sentences of death or even long terms of imprisonment.

'Forgive me asking you, Judge—I expect you get asked this question a lot—but what does it feel like to pass a death sentence?'

'It's always unpleasant to sentence anyone, but one shouldn't take on the job if one isn't prepared to do what is required,' was the judge's usual reply.

He had spent a week in this sort of way without hearing a word from Lesley or Hounds Ltd. and he was beginning to feel and hope that he had perhaps heard the last of the affair, when to his surprise Mr Empton and his wife arrived at the hotel.

'Why, Judge,' said Mr Empton when they first saw each other, 'what a coincidence! How nice to see you.'

'How are you, Empton?' said the judge.

For the first day they kept clear of the subject but it was obvious that this could not go on for ever. When they did start to discuss the case the judge could not help saying:

'One thing that puzzled me was your failure to call Mrs Burford.'

'And well it may, Judge,' said Mr Empton. 'I intended to call her.'

'Yes, I understand that,' said the judge, 'but she told me that later you said you didn't believe her and refused to call her.'

'That I didn't believe her?' said Empton. 'The little liar. I didn't call her because I *did* believe her.'

'I don't understand,' said the judge.

'Well, I suppose that, strictly speaking, I shouldn't tell you, but the case is all over now so far as we are both concerned and it can't really do any harm. I'll tell you why I didn't call her.'

'Why was it?'

'Well, you know that when the police first interviewed him, Burford said that at the time of the robbery he was going for a walk by himself. They didn't say they were asking about the robbery, they just asked him where he was at such a time on such a day. But, later, when they charged him with the robbery, he said he was in bed with his wife. And she confirmed it at first. So, of course, I was going to call her, first to prove Mr Thompson's existence and secondly to prove the alibi.'

'And then what happened?'

'Well, for reasons which don't matter, I thought this was a case where I ought to have a conference with her. During it she let slip that her husband wasn't in bed with

her but that the case seemed so strong against him that
they thought they'd better say they were together, so that
they could have two witnesses instead of him alone.'

'Go on,' said the judge.

'Well, naturally, I put the point to him. He obviously
didn't know what to do. He either had to stick to his guns
or admit that both he and his wife were liars. He decided
to stick to his guns and said his wife's correction was a
mistake. So what was I to do? I obviously couldn't call
her after that, could I, Judge?'

'No, of course not,' said the judge. 'You're quite sure of
all this, I suppose. There's no possibility of a mistake?'

'None at all. She explained to me that, when they saw
the evidence piling up against him and there appeared to
be only his word against so much, it seemed to be the only
thing to do.'

'Then why did she admit it to you?'

'It was an accident, I think. She let something slip, and
I cross-examined her about it. And then it all came out.'

'This fellow Thompson—do you think he exists?'

'Do you, Judge?'

'Well, I confess that, until you gave me this last bit of
information, I was inclined to think he did. But now it's
a very different situation.'

'What always annoys me about these absent villains is
that they always call them by such obvious names. It's
always Brown or Jones or Thompson, or something of that
kind. Why can't they say Montgomery?'

'Or Sugden-Placey,' said the judge. 'A name like that
would certainly carry conviction. I don't mind telling
you, Empton, that I've made a complete fool of myself
over this case. Even more than I thought a few minutes
ago. Heavens, what a fool!'

'I'm sure you haven't really, Judge. It must be very
worrying to think you've made a mistake if a man's life
or liberty depends on it. I'm very glad to have been able
to relieve your mind on the subject.'

'You certainly have in one way,' said the judge, 'but you've raised another problem at the same time.'

He was now wondering whether he should get on to Maclachlan and tell him to cry off the search immediately. He also had to decide what he was to tell Lesley. He couldn't in fact tell her what he'd heard, as Empton shouldn't have given away to anyone what Lesley had said to him. It was a very awkward problem, and, as usual with the judge, the worry began to multiply itself. He had just told Lesley in effect that he believed her story that Thompson existed. How could he suddenly tell her that he didn't without saying why? And, if he simply wrote that he'd changed his mind and was not prepared to help any more, that would be tantamount to doing the same thing. He would like to have consulted Empton on the subject but he did not feel he could.

He had still not made up his mind what to do when he went to the bar for a drink before dinner.

'That was an odd case,' said a fellow guest, 'when you helped to recapture the man you'd sentenced.'

'Yes,' said the judge. 'It was odd.'

'How the fellow must have hated you.'

'What surprises me,' said another, 'is that judges never seem to be attacked by criminals whom they've sentenced. You hear occasional threats from the dock when a man is sentenced, but, when the chap comes out, he never tries to do anything about it.'

'That's as well for us,' said the judge. 'But I suppose it's because they appreciate that we're really doing our duty and that we're quite impersonal and simply representing the public.'

'But,' said another guest, 'one might have thought the relatives of a chap would have a go. Some of them believe passionately in their husband's or father's innocence. This fellow Burford's wife, for instance, has she ever written to you an anonymous threatening letter?'

'Well, if it was anonymous,' said the judge, 'and the

handwriting carefully enough disguised, I couldn't tell, could I? But in fact I've had no threatening or abusive letters from anyone about the case.'

At that moment the receptionist came into the bar.

'Oh, Sir Gerald,' she said, 'there's a lady to see you, a Mrs Burford.'

CHAPTER EIGHTEEN

Interruptions to a Holiday

WITHOUT a clear idea of exactly what he was going to say, the judge went out to see her. One thing he was determined to do and that was to finish the thing off there and then. Embarrassing as her call was, at least it enabled him to deal with the matter at once.

He found her in the hotel front lounge looking excited and almost happy.

'Sir Gerald,' she said, 'I've some wonderful news. I had to come over at once.'

'You have wasted your time,' said the judge, 'and mine.'

She saw how angry he seemed to be.

'I'm terribly sorry to have disturbed you at your hotel,' she said, 'but I really did think it was justified. Do please forgive me.'

'Please say what you want and then go.'

'But Sir Gerald, I don't understand. We've found the man and Mr Maclachlan is keeping an eye on him at the moment.'

'Now, look, Mrs Burford,' said the judge. 'I've had just about enough of this. You've lied to me from the start and I've no doubt you're lying now.'

'I'm not, Sir Gerald, really I'm not.'

'But you have lied to me, haven't you? About your husband's alibi?'

'How do you know?'

'Never mind how I know. It's enough that I do. And that's an end of the whole matter. I wash my hands of it.'

'But Sir Gerald, you must let me explain. We've really

found him again. It would be too dreadful if we had to let him go.'

'You can go to the police.'

'But I have and they say there's nothing they can arrest him for. They won't do anything without your backing.'

'You've had all the help I'm prepared to give.'

'But let me explain, Sir Gerald, about the alibi. I did tell you a lie about that. I didn't give evidence because I wasn't with William. I know it was wrong of us to make it up, but everything was being made up against William and, if evidence is faked on one side, it doesn't seem so bad to do a little in return.'

'Are you suggesting the police faked evidence against you?'

'No, not the police—Thompson.'

'Oh, Thompson,' said the judge. 'I'm a bit tired of him.'

'But do listen to me, Sir Gerald. You've done so much and been so kind. I'm sure you wouldn't let me down now. My husband's in prison for ten years, and there he'll stay without your help. Now that I really have found the man, surely you'll give just that one extra piece of help.'

'You found him at Esher, I believe,' said the judge.

'Yes, I did,' said Lesley. 'Don't you believe me?'

'How can I?' said the judge, 'you lie whenever it suits you. I ought to have realised it from the start.'

'Sir Gerald, I had to lie to you. I was terrified if I told you the truth about the alibi you wouldn't go on helping. Can't you see that? My husband is doing ten years for a crime he didn't commit. I tell you that within six or seven hours I can show you the man who actually committed the crime and planted the evidence on my husband. Are you just going to throw me out because I told a lie? Was it so dreadful to tell that lie? Of course, we shouldn't have done so, but no one would believe William about anything and there seemed no alternative. You've never had a case faked against you, Sir Gerald, you can't know what it means.'

'I'm not sure that I don't,' said the judge.

'Please, Sir Gerald,' said Lesley, 'I will do anything in the world to try to convince you.'

'I believe you'd *say* anything in the world,' said the judge.

'This is our last chance,' said Lesley. 'Please give it us. Surely you give everyone a last chance.'

'Where do you say the man is at the moment?'

'He's at a hotel in Doncaster.'

'Why didn't you telephone?'

'Because I wanted to fetch you.'

'What do the police say?'

'They say there's nothing they can do without some evidence.'

'All right,' said the judge, 'I'll miss my dinner and come with you. I'm probably a fool. In fact I know I am. But you ask for a last chance and you shall have it. I'll get some things. I suppose I shall have to stay the night there.'

The judge went to collect some clothes and on the way back from his room he ran into Empton.

'Hullo, Judge, you going out before dinner?'

'I've been called away suddenly—just for the night.'

'People in the bar were saying that a Mrs Burford had called to see you.'

'People in the bar can say what they like,' said the judge. 'I'm in a hurry.'

But he wondered what they would say when he was away and what he could say when he came back.

He was just about to leave the hotel when he was summoned to the telephone. It was his clerk. A judge who was to have sat in the Court of Criminal Appeal next morning had been taken ill. The Lord Chief Justice would be most grateful if the judge could possibly take his place. It was anticipated that the appeals would only take a day.

'Very well,' said the judge, 'I'll do it.'

A few minutes later he explained to Lesley what had happened.

'I'm sorry,' he said, 'but this must come first. Keep your man under observation the whole time and I will come tomorrow night if the list is finished. You can telephone me at the Law Courts.'

Before he left to catch the last train he saw Empton again.

'In case the people in the bar want to know what I'm doing, I'm going to London to sit in the Court of Criminal Appeal tomorrow.'

'Are you really, Judge?'

'Yes, I am,' said the judge almost angrily. 'You'll probably see a report of it in the papers.'

'Burford isn't appealing again, I suppose—but, no, of course, that would be impossible.'

'Burford and Mrs Burford haven't got anything to do with it,' said the judge.

But they had a good deal to do with the judge on his way to London. It seemed impossible to believe that Lesley wasn't telling the truth this time, and yet once you know people to be liars can you have any trust in them? But what could her object be in getting him to go to Doncaster if she hadn't found the man? What could her object have been in getting him to Esher? She had certainly lied to him, but wasn't there something in her explanation? If she'd admitted having lied, from her point of view, she might have lost the interest of the only person who was prepared to help. Yes, he must give her this last chance.

CHAPTER NINETEEN

The Last Chance

THE last chance is what most criminals get when they appeal to the Court of Criminal Appeal, for, as Mr Justice Carstairs complained, when Mr Empton refused to try to get the Burford case to the House of Lords, a further appeal to that House is impossible in most cases, and the Court of Criminal Appeal is their final fling. And in the bad old days of that Court it was not much of a fling. All that has fortunately now been changed, but in those days it was a nice point whether it took longer to have an appeal dismissed or to obtain a decree in an undefended divorce or *vice versa*.

An appeal would start, somewhat unpropitiously from the point of view of the appellant, with the presiding judge saying in an audible whisper to his neighbour:

'There's nothing in this, is there?'

The other judge would shake his head and then the appeal would begin. It was a little discouraging for counsel who had to open the batting on such a wicket. The question was, perhaps, whether a man should hang or go to prison for many years and an appearance that the appeal was going to be heard, before the judges had made up their minds to dismiss it, would have been some comfort to the appellant. But in those days there usually presided over the Court a judge who had made the solemn pronouncement that justice must not only be done but must manifestly be seen to be done. He was much praised for this admirable and well-worded declaration of the rights of those who come before the Courts. It was just unfort-

unate that of all the judges who functioned at that time he
was himself the one who paid the least attention to the
maxim. It is doubtful if the criminals whose appeals were
dismissed by his Court took much comfort from the fact
that the language of his judgments was exquisitely chosen.
He used few and simple words, admirably arranged and
easily understood. It was a delight for those unconcerned
in a case to listen to him, and even counsel who suffered
under him remembered with respect the brilliant choice
of language with which he tore them to pieces.

The trouble, of course, was that, as he was Lord Chief
Justice, other judges were inclined to take their tone from
him. He was a first-class example of the danger of making
a man Lord Chief Justice until he has proved himself as
a judge. It is an example which, it is hoped by many,
will be remembered for ever.

In those days, after the discouraging preliminaries
between two of the judges to which reference has been
made, the appeal would be opened, and it would proceed
something like this:

COUNSEL: This is an appeal from a conviction before Mr
Justice So-and-So at the Central Criminal Court. The
appellant was convicted of murder. The facts which the
prosecution alleged were—

LORD CHIEF JUSTICE: You may take it that we have all
read the evidence.

COUNSEL: Thank you, my Lord. My Lord the grounds
of appeal are as follows—first——

LORD CHIEF JUSTICE: Which is your best ground?

COUNSEL: Well, my Lord, I would respectfully submit
that the judge never put the appellant's case to the jury.
In support of that, my Lords . . .

MR JUSTICE SPEER: One moment, Mr Hoop. If that's
your best point, why have you put it third in the written
notice of appeal?

COUNSEL: Oh, my Lord, the grounds weren't formu-
lated in order of merit.

E

LORD CHIEF JUSTICE: Did you say merit, Mr Hoop?

COUNSEL: My Lords, I should prefer, if I may, to point out to your Lordships . . .

MR JUSTICE BLENKIRON: Do you really say that the judge never put the appellant's case to the jury? Look at the passage on page 123. 'Now the accused says that he was not there at the time. If you believe that, members of the jury, that is an end of the matter.'

LORD CHIEF JUSTICE: Mr Hoop, do I correctly understand that you settled this notice of appeal?

COUNSEL: Yes, my Lord.

LORD CHIEF JUSTICE: Then will you kindly explain how you came to make that wholly unfounded criticism of the learned judge in view of the passage which my Lord has just read.

COUNSEL: My Lords, you should have heard the way the learned judge said it.

LORD CHIEF JUSTICE: That is a most improper observation for which you will apologise immediately.

COUNSEL: Oh, my Lord, I didn't mean to . . .

LORD CHIEF JUSTICE: You will apologise immediately.

COUNSEL: My Lord, I'm extremely sorry.

LORD CHIEF JUSTICE: Very well then. Have you anything else to add in support of this appeal?

The Lord Chief Justice then ostentatiously picks up the Law List and looks in it. By this he successfully conveys to the lawyers in the Court without saying a word: 'Who is this fellow Hoop?'

Within a further five minutes the appeal is over, the Lord Chief Justice remarking that the only reason the appeal was brought was because it was a case of murder, as though it were rather insulting to their Lordships to have to consider the dull question whether a man should be hanged or not.

Such an unenviable tradition does not die easily, and it was some time before the Court became what it is now, a Court for *hearing* as well as determining appeals.

The cases which came before Mr Justice Carstairs and his brethren were a varied lot, but they were all considered on such merits (if any) as they had. They included a gentleman who had actually been convicted by a jury of being too much under the influence of drink while driving a car, two cases of bigamy, three of false pretences, a robbery with violence and two burglaries.

The Court was presided over by Mr Justice Fairweather, and the third member of the Court was Mr Justice Dalmunzie. He was a Scotsman who had somehow or other found his way on to the English instead of the Scottish Bench. He used to show considerable annoyance when his name was incorrectly pronounced. This could never happen when he was sitting alone as then he was invariably called 'my Lord.' But, when he was sitting with other judges, it might be necessary for Counsel in addressing the Court to say 'as Mr Justice Dalmunzie has said' or something of that kind. Experienced practitioners knew that the 'z' was pronounced more like a 'g' but young and inexperienced barristers could not at first make out why the judge in question spoke tartly to them after they had pronounced his name. He felt as strongly about his name, as many judges feel when the late Mr Justice Lopes' name is pronounced as one syllable to rhyme with ropes instead of two syllables to rhyme with Tropez.

It was quite a relief to Mr Justice Carstairs to have to apply his mind to his ordinary work, and, although it was impossible for him in the intervals of thinking about an appeal not to wonder whether Lesley really had found her man, he was able to concentrate on the matters in hand pretty well.

One of the cases of false pretences was by a Mr Green who conducted his appeal in person.

'I'm not appealing against sentence this time, my Lords,' he began. 'The sentence was very fair as sentences go.'

'What are you appealing against?' asked the presiding judge.

'The whole bag of tricks, if you'll forgive the expression, my Lords,' said Mr Green.

'Now, Green,' said the presiding judge, 'you must behave yourself.'

'I'm sorry, my Lords,' said Mr Green, 'that was a false start, shall I begin again?'

'We shan't hear you at all, unless you talk sense,' said Mr Justice Dalmunzie.

'I see,' said Mr Green gravely. 'Then, if your Lordships will forgive me while I pull myself together—which normally at this stage I've already been told to do—as Mr Justice Dalmunzie has just said . . .'

He pronounced the name with absolute correctness, and he repeated it just to show it wasn't a mistake.

'As Mr Justice Dalmunzie has just said, I must talk sense and that takes a bit of doing, as your Lordships must well know.'

Mr Justice Dalmunzie was so pleased at his name being correctly pronounced from such an unlikely quarter that he decided for himself that he was prepared to let Mr Green have quite a bit of rope. How many counsel, he reflected, took the elementary precaution to ascertain in advance how a judge's name was pronounced?

'Well,' Mr Green continued, 'I'm not saying that the facts didn't look black against me. They did. And, as I've done the same thing before, it was difficult for the judge not to think I'd done it again.'

'Had you?' asked Mr Justice Carstairs.

'Now, my Lord,' said Mr Green, wagging a forefinger towards the judge, 'that would be described by some ignorant people as a leading question. But I know better. It isn't leading at all. It's a perfectly proper question if I may say so with respect. But awkward, my Lord, awkward. But then you wouldn't have been one of the leading cross-examiners in the country if it weren't awkward, would you, my Lord?'

'Talk sense or be quiet,' said Mr Justice Fairweather, who was the only judge Mr Green had not so far done his best to please.

Mr Green, who had in fact far more experience of the criminal courts than many members of the Bar, had made the most careful enquiries about his judges before he appeared. He was delighted to find the key to Dalmunzie's heart, as he never appealed more than once to the vanity of the same judge. He had found nothing for Fairweather, and had decided to wait for an inspiration.

'I'm sorry, my Lord,' said Mr Green, 'I mustn't abuse my position. A fair hearing's all I want. And it's the one thing I know I'll get here. I wouldn't say that to everyone, my Lords.'

'Now, come along, Green,' said Mr Justice Dalmunzie, 'what's your complaint about the trial?'

'It went wrong from the beginning, my Lord. My defence never got going.'

'But what was it?'

'You may well ask, my Lord,' said Mr Green. 'If I hadn't been there myself, I wouldn't have believed it.'

'Wouldn't have believed what?'

'That such a good defence should vanish in front of my own eyes.'

'What was your defence?'

'It was cast-iron, my Lords. It couldn't fail. Only it did. That's what I'm complaining about.'

'But I don't follow,' said Mr Justice Carstairs. 'What was wrong with the trial?'

'Oh, my Lord,' said Mr Green, 'a cast-iron defence shouldn't fail, should it, my Lord? There must be something wrong, if it does.'

'Perhaps what was wrong was that it wasn't cast-iron.'

'That's a point,' said Mr Green. 'That's quite a point. I should like to chew that over, my Lord.'

'Well, we have chewed it over,' said Mr Justice Dalmunzie, 'and I'm afraid it seems to me at any rate that you hadn't any defence.'

'That's how it strikes you, my Lord?' said Mr Green.

'I'm afraid so.'

'And what about you, my Lord? You didn't think that, did you?' said Mr Green, addressing Mr Justice Fairweather.

'Yes, I did.'

'And that only leaves one of you in my favour,' said Mr Green. 'That's terrible.'

'You mustn't make that assumption,' said Mr Justice Carstairs. 'For the moment I'm against you too.'

'Oh dear!' said Mr Green, 'then I'll have to begin all over again.'

It was not long, however, before the Court felt compelled to dismiss Mr Green's appeal. He thanked them all for a most courteous hearing.

'Better luck next time, Green,' said Mr Justice Dalmunzie.

'Next time, my Lord?' said Mr Green, with affected pain in his voice. 'I'm going straight in future—if I can remember which direction that is.'

During the lunch adjournment they were discussing Mr Green's case, when Mr Justice Dalmunzie said to Mr Justice Carstairs:

'You know, it's a pity about that chap. There's a lot of good in him and he's got a great sense of fun. Most criminals are dull dogs. If someone could have given him a helping hand early in his career he might have had a very different life.'

'Could very well be.'

'Have you ever followed up a case and tried to help the fellow?'

'I can't say that I have,' began Mr Justice Carstairs. 'Well, not in the sense you mean. As a matter of fact, I have been trying to help a man get rid of a conviction.'

'Oh, Burford—yes, I've heard all about that,' said Mr Justice Dalmunzie.

'What's your view?' said the judge.

'D'you really want it?'

'Of course.'

'Well, I'm a dour Scotsman, but I think you must be mad. Haven't I heard that you've been up and down the country staying in hotels with the man's beautiful wife?'

'Certainly not,' said the judge. 'I've been to a few race-meetings with her—that's all. And I did once go on a wild goose chase to Esher, and as a matter of fact I'm going on another tonight.'

'Well the rumours weren't so far wrong then. But, if you want my advice, you'll get out of it quick. Women like that can be very dangerous. She might even try to blackmail you.'

'Whatever for?'

'Oh, nothing, of course. But if I were you I should keep my bedroom door locked when you go on one of your wild goose chases.'

'But, if you thought a man was innocent, wouldn't you do anything about it?'

'Of course I would. But it wouldn't entail going out with the innocent man's wife. We'll all be inviting Mr Green to dinner at the club at this rate.'

'That's completely different. He's just a comic crook. This man Burford's doing ten years and may be innocent.'

'May be?'

'Yes, of course, it's only "may be" but wouldn't that be enough for you to want to do something?'

'I've already said "Yes"—but not what you're doing. However, as I said, I'm a dour Scotsman, and we're rather inclined to keep our energies for causes which haven't been lost. They're more productive.'

It was this kind of conversation which strengthened the judge in his determination to give the Burfords this one final chance. Although he felt far from certain in the matter having regard to the lies which Lesley had told him, he couldn't really see how she could just be pretending this time. He hoped the list would end early so that he could get to Doncaster as quickly as possible and get things over one way or the other. For that reason he personally would not have given Mr Green as much latitude as his colleagues were prepared to give.

In the afternoon they dealt with the motorist. His complaint was a simple one.

'My Lord,' said counsel on his behalf, 'when my client was first examined by the doctor at the police station, he asked for a blood test. It was refused.'

'Why was that?' asked Mr Justice Fairweather.

'I cannot do better than give the doctor's own answer. "Because," he said, "the accused was obviously drunk and it wasn't necessary."'

'How do you know that a person is obviously drunk?' asked Mr Justice Dalmunzie.

'Exactly, my Lord,' said counsel. 'That was my point. The doctor said he applied the usual tests and the appellant failed every one of them. He couldn't walk straight, he couldn't spell properly, his speech was slurred, his eyes were glazed, his tongue furry and his breath smelled strongly of alcohol. In addition he insisted on calling everyone "darling", though he was not an Irishman. I put to the doctor that any one of his symptoms, with a single exception, could have been due to causes other than drink. The doctor agreed. He even added that it was possible, though not likely, that they could all occur at the same time in the same person. The one reason that he refused to apply a blood test was because, in addition to the symptoms which could theoretically have been accounted for by something other than too much alcohol, his breath, so it was said, smelled strongly of alcohol.'

'Well, so far,' said Mr Justice Fairweather, 'I don't know what you're complaining about.'

'My client said then, and he maintains now, that his

breath nearly always smells of alcohol even though he has
taken none for twenty four hours. He is even ready to
prove it to your Lordships now. He has been in custody for
the past twenty four hours and he would like to demon-
strate to your Lordships that his breath smells strongly of
alcohol now.'

'Perhaps he took in such a quantity before surrendering
to his bail that it is still effective,' said Mr Justice Fairweather.

'Well,' said Mr Justice Dalmunzie, 'I for one am not
going to smell the appellant's breath.'

'I certainly cannot smell anything from here,' said Mr
Justice Fairweather, turning his head towards the prisoner
who was about seven yards away.

'You should have offered the jury the opportunity,'
said Mr Justice Carstairs.

'We did,' said counsel, 'and that is one of the grounds
of appeal, that the judge would not permit it. He said that
he could not allow evidence to be given to the jury which
was not also given to him. And the learned judge took the
same view as Mr Justice Dalmunzie.' Counsel pronounced
the 'z' as he spoke the name of the judge.

'The learned judge was perfectly right,' said that judge,
showing a trace of annoyance in his voice. 'A judge is not
a witness, nor is a jury.'

'But they have a view sometimes,' said counsel. 'Why
not a smell?'

'At any rate,' said Mr Justice Carstairs, 'the judges at
the Central Criminal Court would have an advantage
over us. They have nosegays. Did you suggest to the
learned judge that one of the Sheriffs' nosegays might be
passed round the jury after the test? The judge could have
used his own.'

'I'm afraid not, my Lord.'

'Did you call evidence to prove that the appellant's
breath always smelled of alcohol although he had not been
drinking?'

'His wife and two children, my Lord.'

'Poor things,' said Mr Justice Fairweather. 'But I suppose they get used to it. But did you not have tests made before the trial to prove your point?'

'No, my Lord.'

'Why not? It was the obvious thing to do. If you could have shown that, although a test would prove that the appellant had no alcohol in his blood, his breath nevertheless smelled strongly of alcohol, that would have gone some way to make good your point.'

'Well, my Lord, if your Lordships would allow further evidence, that could still be done,' said counsel.

'But how can we?' said Mr Justice Fairweather. 'We cannot make ourselves into a jury. And even your test, if successful from your point of view, would not prove your case conclusively. Your client's breath could have smelled of alcohol for one of two reasons, either the usual one because he had recently taken some or because he had some special affection or whatever you like to call it which caused the smell to linger about him long after the liquid itself had left his blood stream. Now the jury could—I only say could—have given your client the benefit of the doubt if satisfied by the test, but we couldn't possibly do so.'

'You should have prepared your case better,' said Mr Justice Dalmunzie. 'Before you go into Court there are several things that a wise advocate should do—for example, learn how to pronounce the names—the names of any cases he may be going to cite and so forth. But, if he fails to take any of these precautions, that is not a good ground of appeal.'

'But, my Lord, it could have done no harm for the doctor to make the test,' said counsel.

'No doubt,' said Mr Justice Fairweather, 'you urged that on the jury.'

'My Lord, it's true that I did. But I do urge on your Lordships the undesirability of this case being finally

decided without my client being given a proper chance to
prove this point. Would your Lordships not even let the
usher smell the appellant's breath, or better still the
warder sitting next to him.'

'Well,' said Mr Justice Fairweather to the warder,
'does the appellant's breath smell of alcohol?'

The warder went very red in the face.

'I'm afraid, my Lord,' he said, 'I've only just come on
duty and I had a glass of beer with my lunch.'

Shortly afterwards the appeal was dismissed and the
Court went on to consider the case of the next appellant
whose name, unfortunately for Mr Justice Carstairs, was
Thompson. It pulled him up with a jerk and he looked at
the clock. The appellant had been charged with burglary
and his defence was an alibi.

'Just up your street,' whispered the presiding judge to
Mr Justice Carstairs. The judge gave a slight grin but it
was not a happy one. He hoped it looked better than it
felt.

There was ample evidence against the accused, but he
claimed, just as William had claimed, that he was in bed
with his wife.

'Why is it,' whispered the presiding judge to Mr
Justice Dalmunzie, 'that burglars are always so affection-
ate?'

'Because they work at night,' replied his colleague.

It transpired that the short ground of appeal was that,
although in this case the wife had given evidence to
support her husband's alibi, the judge's summing up had
hardly referred to the matter, and had then done so in a
manner most prejudicial to the appellant.

'It is true,' he had said, 'that the prisoner's wife has said
on oath that the prisoner was with her at the material
time but one can have some sympathy with a wife who
feels compelled to support her husband's story in such
circumstances.'

'I must say,' said Mr Justice Carstairs, 'that, for myself,

I think that was a most unfortunate way in which to refer to the woman's evidence. It was a clear suggestion that she was committing perjury. That was for the jury to say.'

'I respectfully agree, my Lord,' said counsel. 'Her evidence was entitled to as much consideration as anyone else's, and it was pushed aside with what I hope I may term, without disrespect to the learned judge, a sympathetic sneer.'

'Your trouble,' said Mr Justice Fairweather, 'is this, isn't it? Had the evidence of the appellant's wife been put properly to the jury, as I agree with you it ought to have been, could the jury in the light of the rest of the evidence have returned any other verdict? Although I think we all agree that the learned judge was in error in treating her evidence as he did, were not the jury bound, or almost bound, to come to the conclusion they came to in view of the case for the prosecution?'

'If your Lordship says "almost bound," that is surely sufficient for my purposes,' said counsel. 'Unless they were bound to find my client guilty the judge's summing up may have unfairly led them to a verdict which they might not otherwise have given.'

'We think we should like to hear what the prosecution says about this,' said Mr Justice Fairweather.

'What I say is this,' said counsel for the prosecution. 'The case against the accused was about as formidable as such a case can be. The accused was questioned twelve hours after the burglary and was found to be in possession of articles which were undoubtedly stolen at the time of the burglary. At first he would give no explanation. Then he said he found them. Found a bicycle pump, a spanner and a spare bicycle wheel in good condition. Of course, my Lords, if the word "found" is used in the sense in which I believe it has sometimes been used in the Army, I do not criticise the appellant's answer. Later, however, he said that he had not found them but that they'd been sold to him by a man whose name he didn't know, for a

price he couldn't remember. Apparently he wanted to
buy a bicycle pump and a spare wheel when he hadn't a
bicycle. He said he was thinking of getting a
bicycle.'

'But you say he stole them,' said Mr Justice Fairweather. 'What *did* he want them for?'

'Oh, my Lord,' said counsel, 'it must have been in your
Lordship's experience that, if you burgle a place, there
may unfortunately be nothing worth taking but you don't
like to have nothing for your pains, so you take whatever
you can, even if you have no real need for it.'

'I can assure you I don't,' said Mr Justice Fairweather.

'I apologise, my Lord. I put it badly.'

'You put it very well,' said Mr Justice Fairweather,
'but in the wrong direction.'

'Thank you, my Lord. And I may add that those
articles, although not of much use, could be sold. You
would get—I mean he could get, my Lord, a few shillings
at least for them.'

'What troubles me,' said Mr Justice Carstairs, 'is the
lack of appearance of justice in this case. I agree that there
was a very strong case against the appellant, but, unless
we abolish trials in such cases, the accused must be tried
fairly. It becomes little more than the pretence of a trial
if a judge simply laughs a defence out of Court. The whole
object of a trial is to put the matter into the hands of the
jury. Naturally they may be greatly affected by what the
judge says, and, if he says in effect that evidence can be
disregarded, I imagine that most jurymen might say to
themselves—well, the judge is used to these cases, if he
says "disregard it" it's better to do so. That's possible,
isn't it?'

'Yes, certainly, my Lord.'

'Well, then, isn't it making a farce of the trial? You
offer the prisoner the right of going into the witness box
and calling his wife to support his case and you then tell

the jury to take no notice of what they say. It's true that the learned judge didn't say that about the appellant's evidence, but the principle is just the same if he says it about his wife's.'

'In my submission the jury were bound to convict anyway, my Lord, whatever the judge said,' urged counsel.

'Then he might just as well not have been tried,' said Mr Justice Carstairs.

'My Lord,' said prosecuting counsel, 'there must be a lot of cases where, having regard to the evidence, no jury could properly acquit, but nevertheless the man must be tried if he pleads not guilty.'

'Precisely,' said Mr Justice Carstairs. 'He must be tried and tried fairly. Who am I, or who are you, to say that a jury *must* convict? That is usurping their province. It is perfectly true that there are such things as perverse verdicts but that isn't the right way to approach the conduct of a trial. Should a judge say to himself: "In case this jury is perverse, I will sum up unfairly so as to make sure of a verdict of guilty"?'

'Of course not, my Lord.'

'Then, I confess, I don't know why in this case the learned judge did not put the defence and *all* the evidence in support of it fairly before the jury. He put the evidence for the prosecution fairly enough. It's true this appellant has a very bad record and, if I had to give my personal opinion, I should think he was probably guilty of the crime with which he was charged, but he was entitled to plead not guilty and have the case proved against him and he was entitled to be tried fairly.'

It will be seen that there is no stronger critic of some other judge's unfairness than a judge who is himself normally unfair. In view of the harassing mental experiences which he had recently had, it did cross Mr Justice Carstairs' mind, as he belaboured the judge who had presided at the burglar's trial, that he was perhaps expressing himself more freely because of his own shortcomings. And for one brief moment he wondered whether the judge in question would suddenly have a revulsion of feeling as he had had. But, no doubt quite rightly, he soon dismissed the notion. 'What are they worrying about?' the other judge would say. 'The chap was as guilty as he could be.' But those, he thought, are just the cases you have to watch. Everyone watches the doubtful cases. It's the 'clear' cases where injustice may be done. Cases where a man has many previous convictions, like the burglar, or perhaps one only, like William Burford. Yes, this case was an object lesson to him. No doubt the burglar was guilty but you can't try people like that, or occasionally someone, who has all the appearances against him, will be convicted when he should be acquitted.

'For my part,' he said aloud, continuing his thoughts, 'I do not see how you can successfully urge that there has been no miscarriage of justice. The appellant swore he did not commit the crime and that he was with his wife at the time. His wife confirmed that story. That defence ought to have been put fairly and squarely to the jury without what I may describe as a judicial smirk.'

The other two members of the Court said something to themselves about pots calling kettles black, but they felt, as Mr Justice Carstairs felt, that this summing up just would not do. They allowed the burglar's appeal and set him free to burgle again until he was caught again. But they did not put it that way to the burglar.

'You have a deplorable record,' said Mr Justice Fairweather in announcing the judgment of the Court. 'See that you take full advantage of what has happened today.'

'I will, my Lord,' said the burglar and almost meant it. It is not often that you get clean out of a seven-year sentence.

As Mr Justice Carstairs hurried to the train he thought he caught a glimpse of the burglar and his wife hurrying into a tea shop to celebrate. He was quite wrong in fact, as he should have realised. Burglars seldom celebrate on tea. But it made him for a moment think of the joy that would be in Lesley's face if her William were let out of prison. He caught the train without the slightest hesitation.

CHAPTER TWENTY

Mr Thompson Again

B UT on the way in the train the judge began to have doubts again. What was it that Dalmunzie had said? Blackmail? Keep your bedroom door locked. Ridiculous. Yet was it? What did he know of the Burfords? A previous conviction for receiving stolen goods wasn't much of a reference. And now he had actually started to give her money. Not very much it was true and the larger expense he was paying direct to Hounds Ltd. No, he was being too suspicious. Anyway he would soon know now.

Then he thought about the trial again. Had he really been so unfair? Not as bad as the judge who tried the burglar. That was rather a nice phrase he'd used about him—'a judicial smirk.' And yet wasn't he regularly guilty of the same kind of thing himself? He knew he was. Much better to admit it and turn over a new leaf. It was not too late. It was a tremendous responsibility being a judge. He'd always realised it in a way, but obviously not sufficiently. It was certainly Burford's case which had brought it home to him, and, oddly enough, this burglar's as well. One mustn't be too sentimental about it but it was a satisfying thought to see the man reunited to his wife. Even if it were only for a few weeks.

Yes, one thing was certain. Whatever the result of his journey now, he would be a very different judge in the future. Patient, tolerant, quiet and above all fair. How easy it should be, now that it was brought home to him. And, apart from the good which it would do, he would be so much happier himself. And, of course, he would find everything much less worrying. Probably it was his unconscious instinct that he was a bad judge which made him worry so much. Well, that was all done with. With these comforting thoughts he went to sleep and only woke up shortly before his arrival at Doncaster.

Lesley was there to meet him.

'How good of you to come,' she said.

'I'm not too late?' he asked. 'The bird hasn't flown again?'

'No, it's all right—I think.'

'You think? Then something has happened.'

They were standing by a taxi.

'No. Please jump in.'

Her tone was urgent.

'Very well.'

They got in the taxi and it drove off.

'Hadn't we better call at the police station and fetch an officer?' he suggested.

Lesley hesitated.

'Yes, I suppose we'd better.'

He spoke to the driver:

'Go to the police station first, please.'

As soon as they arrived there the judge got quickly out and was soon interviewing a police inspector. He explained who he was.

'Yes, sir, we've already been told about this matter,' said the inspector, 'but I'm not exactly sure what you want us to do.'

'The situation is this,' said the judge. 'This man Thompson is said by Burford and his wife to have planted the evidence on him. Pound notes handed over, dust somehow put in his trouser turn-ups. Now I must confess that at the trial I didn't believe the man existed and the jury didn't believe it either.'

'Quite so, sir.'

'Now, if it can be proved that he does exist, that fact by

itself is material in which the Home Office may be interested.'

'But that could be ascertained by Mrs Burford looking at him, sir, couldn't it?'

'Really, Inspector!' said the judge, 'Mrs Burford is the wife of the convicted man. Naturally her identification of the man should be corroborated by an independent police officer.'

'Yes, I see that, sir. Well, that's easily arranged.'

'And apart from that, it is highly desirable that the man should be questioned. If he is completely innocent in the matter, he will come to no harm. If he was a party to the robbery you are perfectly entitled to question him.'

'But he isn't bound to answer, sir.'

'I dare say not, Inspector,' said the judge, 'but how many times have I read in the paper that a man has been taken to the police station for questioning?'

'But, if you'll forgive my saying so, sir, I have also read that judges have condemned this procedure as totally illegal. No one, I understand, sir, is bound to answer questions and no one is bound to go to a police station unless he is arrested.'

'You may take it I know the law, Inspector,' said the judge. 'I also know the practice of the police. If you are not prepared to help when I tell you the matter may be of the greatest importance, please say so.'

'Of course, I'm prepared to help, sir, and I'll send an officer with you right away. I was only very respectfully pointing out the limitation of our powers in the matter.'

Ten minutes later the judge and Lesley and a policeman were on their way to the hotel. Mr Maclachlan was standing outside when they arrived.

'I'm terribly sorry about this, Sir Gerald,' he said, as soon as the judge got out.

'What d'you mean?' said the judge.

'Hasn't Mrs Burford told you?'

The judge looked at Lesley.

'So he's gone again, has he?'

Lesley said nothing for a moment.

'If you'll come inside, I'll explain. I suppose the police officer had better go back to the station.'

'I suppose so.'

'Very well then,' said the judge. 'Thank you officer. I'm sorry you've been troubled. Please apologise to the inspector for me for your wasted journey.'

The policeman returned to the police station and the judge and Lesley and Mr Maclachlan went into the hotel.

'It's most unfortunate,' said Mr Maclachlan. 'I had to go off duty for five minutes and left Mrs Burford watching him. And if he hadn't to go and pay his bill and leave in that five minutes!'

'Did you see him yourself?' asked the judge.

'Of course.'

'What did he look like?'

'Much as you'd told me.'

'What name is he using at the hotel?'

'Warren.'

'Not Thompson or Wilson?'

'No, Warren.'

'Where's he gone?'

'We don't know.'

'Has he left no forwarding address?'

'No.'

'Why didn't you tell me this at the station?' the judge said to Lesley.

'I was afraid you'd go straight back. I wanted to prove to you the man existed.'

'You've proved nothing. Why even the police have never seen the man. They haven't, have they?'

'No. They wouldn't do anything without you. But Mr Maclachlan has seen him.'

'Mr Maclachlan has seen a man you pointed out to him, a man whose whereabouts are unknown and who registered here under the name of Warren. That proves precisely nothing. You might have pointed out any man, as far as Mr Maclachlan could tell. That man over there, for example. That's right, isn't it, Mr Maclachlan? All you know is that you were watching a man whom Mrs Burford pointed out to you. That's right, isn't it?'

'Yes, sir, I'm afraid it is.'

'Well, I'm sorry you've had so much trouble for nothing, Mr Maclachlan. I'm sorrier still that I have.'

'I'm afraid it isn't for nothing,' said Mr Maclachlan.

'No, of course not,' said the judge. 'It's not your fault and of course you'll be paid. Now I'm going home.'

'I'm afraid the last train has gone, Sir Gerald.'

'Damnation!' said the judge. 'I'm sorry, but I'm really angry. I suppose I shall have to get a room here.'

He walked up to the desk followed by Lesley and Mr Maclachlan.

'Have you a room for the night?' he asked the receptionist.

'Twin-bedded, sir?'

'Certainly not, I want a single room.'

'I'm so sorry, sir, I thought madam was with you. Yes, we have a room, sir.'

'I'd like to go to it at once, please.'

'Certainly, sir. The porter will take you.'

'Good night,' said the judge curtly to Lesley and Mr Maclachlan. 'Please send your bill in in due course,' he added to Mr Maclachlan.

He went angrily to his room, undressed angrily, got into bed angrily and actually went to sleep angrily. He was awakened by someone coming into his room.

'Who's that?' he called.

It was Lesley and she said so.

'Go away at once, please,' he said.

'I must speak to you,' she said and turned on the light. She was in pyjamas and a dressing-gown.

'I couldn't sleep,' she said.

'Well, I could. Please go away.'

He suddenly remembered Dalmunzie's advice. He wished he'd taken it.

'You must please listen to me. I'm so terribly unhappy.'

'I dare say you are, but I can't help you any more.'

'Are you being quite fair?' said Lesley. 'Everything I've told you has been true.'

'It's been nothing of the sort. You deliberately lied to me at the station.'

'Oh, that,' said Lesley, 'yes, I'm sorry about that. But I had to do it or you'd have gone home.'

'I certainly would. Now will you please leave me or I shall ring the bell.'

'Please listen to me first. I am sorry about lying to you again but it's not my fault that the man went off. If it hadn't been for that beastly Court you went to, he'd have still been here.'

'He always has to wait till I'm about ten yards off. Then he disappears.'

'That really isn't my fault. We found him at Doncaster races and followed him here. We've kept him under observation between us ever since. But you must realise I couldn't let him see me, or he might take fright and go abroad for a bit. He can't know he's being followed at the moment and it's vital he shouldn't. Can you imagine my feelings when I had to let him go, knowing you were on the way up here?'

'Can you imagine mine when I was told he'd gone?'

'Of course, I can, but is it fair of you to blame me for it? I thought judges were always fair. You came up to Doncaster because you believed you might see the man and get the police to make enquiries about him, didn't you?'

'Yes,' said the judge grudgingly.

'Well, what has happened to make you decide that that can't still happen? We've been to the police and Maclachlan saw the man himself. Why should I go to all that trouble unless it were true? What possible object could I have?'

'How can I tell what are the objects of a person who deliberately lies to someone who is helping her?'

'Oh, please, please, Sir Gerald, don't give us up. You're our only hope.'

And Lesley burst into tears and put herself in the judge's arms. For a moment the judge wondered if the door would suddenly open and a man demand what he was doing with his wife. Blackmail. Keep your door locked.

But the door did not open and Lesley remained sobbing on his chest.

'There, there,' he said and patted her back.

It was a silly thing to do because at the third pat his hand stayed there for a moment or two and, being a normal man, he could not help realising even more than he had before that Lesley was an extremely attractive young woman. And she was in his room. On his bed. At the same moment he realised that High Court judges did not usually receive the wives of convicted felons on their beds, even fully dressed. And Lesley wasn't.

'Now, please,' he said. 'This won't do. You must sit up.'

Lesley sat up and for a split second the judge almost regretted it.

She looked him full in the eyes and said:

'Please.'

Usually in such circumstances it is the man who is saying: Please.

'I'm sorry,' he said. 'I quite see your point of view, and I was annoyed and perhaps a little hasty. But I really can't go running up and down the country any more.'

'But if I find him again? And I'm sure we shall now. He obviously feels things have blown over and that the police have got their scapegoat in William. He thinks they won't be looking for anyone else. He'll turn up again.'

'Then you must go to the police. Tell them everything you know and ask for their help.'

'We won't get far without you to back us.'

The judge remembered that even with his help the police had not been particularly co-operative.

'I suppose,' he said, 'it is the same man as you saw at Esher?'

'Of course it is. Do you still disbelieve the whole story?'

'To be frank, I just don't know what to believe. What address did Warren register in the hotel book?'

'Another hotel. In Blackpool.'

'Well, enquiries can be made there.'

'I expect it'll be hotels all the way along and he won't have stayed at the last one. Or just a non-existent address.'

'You seem to know all about this sort of thing.'

'I'm only using my imagination. Isn't that what a crook would do?'

'I thought you said he didn't think he was being followed.'

'Even so, he wouldn't give away anything unnecessarily. You may not think you are being followed, but you don't advertise how you can be found, do you?'

'As he's going round race-meetings so much surely there must be people who know where he is. Bookmakers or people like that?'

'I expect he does any betting in cash.'

'Tell me something completely different. Why did both you and your husband at first suggest that this man and your husband had been at school together, St James's wasn't it?'

'It was just a mistake.'

'It was St James's, wasn't it?'

'Yes, but you're not going there, are you?'

'Why are you so anxious that I shouldn't?'

'Oh, nothing, really. There's no point in it. Besides we

naturally didn't want William's second conviction advertised too much.'

'But they must know of it?'

'I suppose so, but don't go there, will you? It can only hurt us.'

'At the moment,' said the judge, 'I don't propose to go anywhere—except to sleep, if you'll let me. But I'll see you in the morning. Now go back to your room, there's a good girl. I really am sorry for you, and, if there's anything I can do to help which doesn't entail wild-goose chases up and down the country, I will. For instance, if you find him again I'll speak to the police on the telephone. That should be just as good. They can check the authenticity of the call.'

'Oh, you are good,' she said and kissed him quickly on the forehead. Then she left.

But the judge did not sleep this time. His worrying apparatus came swiftly into action. There was no doubt that Lesley lied when it suited her but, on consideration of everything that had happened, he could not think of any motive for her behaviour except possibly revenge. And that really seemed futile. So he finally decided that he would help her in the way he had indicated but that he would not undertake any further long journeys and he certainly would not stay again at the same hotel as Lesley. He also decided that he would pay a visit to the headmaster of St James's, which was quite near London, but he did not propose to tell Lesley of this intention.

CHAPTER TWENTY-ONE

Interview with a Headmaster

ABOUT a fortnight later he wrote to the headmaster for an interview and was given an appointment. Henry Sprout, the headmaster, was a remarkable man. He had left school at the age of fourteen completely untaught. Always near the bottom of his class, he had failed in every examination which he had taken, however simple. So far from complaining at his behaviour his parents encouraged him. The sooner he was out and earning, the better. There was always a danger that, if a boy did well, they would keep him at school, like Henry's elder brother Alfred. Alfred was always held up to Henry as an example of what not to do. Alfred had been forced to go into a Grammar School and even to a University. He ended up as a librarian with £600 a year at the age of twenty-four. Eight or nine years wasted when he might have been earning an average over the years of at least £9 or £10 a week. Several thousand pounds lost to the family. It was like failing to post a winning line on a pools coupon. Horrible.

So Henry was the blue-eyed boy of the family and his parents gloated over such reports on his progress as: 'Might do a little better if he tried.' 'Good boy,' his father would say, 'there won't be no flippin' grammar schools for you.'

But as soon as he left school and started to earn £4 a week as a boy in a garage Henry acquired a thirst for knowledge. It was not simply his parents' encouragement which had prevented him from learning at school. It was the method of teaching which he could not stand. He was an obstinate person and resisted strongly anything to which he objected. But, as soon as the shackles were removed, the qualities in his mind which had shown themselves to a limited degree in his brother Alfred began to make themselves felt and at a very rapid rate. He began to read voraciously. And the more he learned the more he wanted to learn. The boy who resisted all efforts to teach him at his elementary school voluntarily attended night school. And not only that. He soon started to show himself to be head and shoulders above the other students in his capacity to learn. There were still, of course, huge gaps in his knowledge, and he would sometimes startle his teachers as much by his ignorance as by his memory.

His parents had now no objection to his attending school. Henry was earning and it was much better in fact to know that he was at night school or reading at home than to wonder whether he might become involved with young hooligans or, almost as bad, whether one day he might inform them that unfortunately by pure accident and without really meaning it his girl friend Elsie was going to have a baby. No, Henry remained the blue-eyed boy, earning steadily and increasingly and leading a quiet, respectable life.

About ten years after he had left school Henry was lying under a car in the ordinary course of his work when it suddenly occurred to him that he was wasting his time. He was now a very well-educated young man, though still with occasional odd gaps in his knowledge which were even rather attractive, like one untidy curl in exceptionally pretty hair.

His parents were at first alarmed when he told them his plans, but, as the plan included a period of intensive work at the garage during which he proposed to save enough to enable him to give up work for the purpose of getting a degree, they did not make too much fuss about it. And indeed, they knew it would be useless, for Henry was twenty-four and quite capable of looking after himself.

At the age of thirty Henry, complete with the necessary qualifications, obtained his first teaching job. He at once showed himself to be a born teacher. He applied the methods which he would have liked to have been applied to himself. He had a complete mistrust of examinations, but he realised that, as long as the system of examinations continued, he would have to get his pupils through them. But, as far as possible, he concentrated on creating in his pupils a desire to know.

Henry's father and grandfather had come from Bermondsey and Henry had been brought up to talk as they did. As he began to associate with more educated people he started to acquire a more cultured accent and method of speech, and, as he had a particularly musical ear, it was only a few years before he could talk almost perfect English. On the other hand, he could relapse, whenever he wanted, into his original dialect, just as many Scotsmen who can speak perfect English without a trace of Scottish accent can also speak the broadest Scotch. Henry could speak rhyming slang and back slang, and he had a complete Cockney vocabulary at his command, and on occasion he found it was most effective with his class. He would, for example, sometimes introduce a subject like this:

'Yer put the x's up on the board and yer put the brackets arahnd 'em.'

It was not long before Henry's flair for teaching made itself felt and he gradually acquired better and better jobs, ending up with the headmastership of St James's. He was immensely successful as a headmaster and his sense of mischief, which sometimes induced him to shock some of the parents, was an asset rather than the reverse. On one occasion, for example, when the parents were attending some school function immaculately dressed, many of them in morning coats and grey top hats, Henry greeted them in his shirtsleeves. 'Sorry,' he said. 'Forgot me tie.'

This sort of behaviour would never have been tolerated in a lesser man, but parents whose sons were guaranteed as good an education as you can get in the country could afford to be amused at some of his antics and to leave their sons quite confidently in his charge.

One of Henry's pet aversions was pomposity, and it was dangerous to give yourself airs in his presence, either as a parent or a pupil.

'Wot's yer farver, Spriggs?' he said one day when he thought the form needed a little uplift.

'A schoolmaster, sir.'

'Tell 'im to come in a bowler 'at next time. The monkey should stick to 'is tree. Now we'll do some 'omer. 'Ow many of you don't know the first three books of the *Iliad* by 'eart?'

All the boys' hands went up.

'Well, yer will by the end of term or there won't be no end of term.'

It was on this remarkable man that the judge called. Unfortunately for him Henry Sprout had a particular dislike for judges. This was partly due to his dislike of pomposity, which he always associated with the judiciary. Partly also it was probably due to an innate dislike of the successors of men who had sent some of his forbears to prison. The judge, however, was wholly unaware of the character of the man whom he was going to interview. He drove up to the school and, as he got out of his car, the headmaster in his shirtsleeves, approached him.

'I've an appointment with the headmaster,' he said.

'Well, yer late.'

'I am not,' said the judge, 'and, even if I were, there's no need to be rude about it.'

'Do yer know 'oo yer talking to?' said the headmaster.

'I'm afraid not, except that it's someone who ought to learn some manners.'

'It's you wot's going to learn. This wye.'

The headmaster led the judge into the school and along several corridors. On the way they met some of the boys who appeared to treat the judge with the utmost deference. 'Nice-mannered boys,' he thought, 'they can't know who I am. If the teaching is as good as their behaviour it must be a first-class place.'

Eventually they reached a room. The headmaster opened the door.

'In yer go,' he said, 'and sit down. People say make yerself at 'ome, but 'ow you do that with a 'ard uncomfortable chair like this one I just dunno. Still it's all yours.'

The judge sat down opposite a desk and to his amazement the headmaster went and sat in his own chair facing the judge across the desk. Well, it was not his business how the school servants behaved, though he certainly proposed to report this man for his rudeness.

'Will the headmaster be long?' he asked.

'Not longer than I can 'elp,' said Mr Sprout. 'Wotcher want?'

'I'll tell that to the headmaster.'

'That's wot I've arst yer to do.'

The judge decided that silence was the only dignified weapon he could use.

'Come on,' said Mr Sprout, 'cough it up.'

'Will you kindly tell the headmaster that I'm here,' said the judge angrily.

''E knows,' said Mr Sprout. ''E's a-looking at you at this werry moment.'

The judge looked around the room to see if there were any hatchways or spyholes but could not see any. There was another door to the room and he could only imagine the headmaster was looking at him through the keyhole. Extraordinary behaviour, he thought.

'You're a judge, ain't yer? Don't seem very quick off the mark.'

'I shall report you to the headmaster,' said the judge.

'That's just wot you're a-doing of.'

'Don't be absurd,' said the judge.

''Oo d'yer think this room belongs to?'

'The headmaster.'

'Right. And this chair?'

'The headmaster.'

'Right. Go up top. And wot am I doing in it?'

'I haven't the faintest idea,' said the judge.

'Go down again,' said Mr Sprout.

'Now, look,' said the judge, 'I've had enough of this tomfoolery.'

'That's O.K.,' said the headmaster. 'If you've 'ad all yer want, yer know yer way out.'

'Where is the headmaster?' said the judge loudly and angrily, in the faint hope that, if he were anywhere near, the headmaster would hear him.

'Yer 'oped 'e'd 'ear that, didn't yer? Well 'e did, if yer wanter know.'

'Please tell me where he is.'

''Ere.'

'What d'you mean?'

'It's me. D'yer mind?'

The judge thought for a moment or two.

'Are you telling me that you are the headmaster?'

'I am. And sober, too,' he added, anticipating the judge's next question, which he could not quite stop.

'Are you . . .'

'I just tole yer. Stone cold sober. Never touch a drop before the eleven break.'

'You're the headmaster of this school?' asked the judge incredulously.

'Look, chum,' said the headmaster. 'I ain't taking no offence at the presink. A lotter people don't reckernise me first go. Now I only 'ave to tell my boys a thing wunst. I won't say blokes like you don't need it twice. And I won't say no to wunce more. But if yer ask again after three times, them's fighting words in these 'ere parts.'

And the headmaster jumped up, got into a fighting

position and, after sparring for a moment or two, knocked out an imaginary opponent. 'One, two, three,' he began. 'Out' he added. 'Satisfied?' he asked while the judge was still trying to take in this astonishing performance.

'I suppose you're saying to yerself, 'ow can a bloke like 'im run a school like this. It don't make sense. Well, yer wrong, it do. Take a dekko at this.'

The headmaster went across to a wall and pulled up a blind which disclosed a table.

'O level,' he announced proudly. 'A 'undred and fifty entrants. A 'undred with eight subjicts, thirty-seven with seven, eight with six, four with five and one little basket with only three. No failyers. Can they beat that at 'Arrer? Not, mind yer, that I think a lot o' this way of eddication. I don't 'old with it at all. I didn't 'ave no O and A levels. I learned 'cos I wanted to. And that's the only way. I could teach 'em so that they really 'eld the knowledge and wanted more. 'Course, yer got to 'ave a system. But this crammin' ain't it. Got yer breaf back yet, Dad?'

The judge was still gaping.

'Orl right,' said the headmaster. 'Take it easy now. 'Ere's A level. Wotcher think o' that?'

He went to another blind on the wall and raised it.

'Seventy eight candidits, no failyers. One with four subjicts, sixty-five with three, eleven with two and one with one. 'E was the brother of the other little basket. I'd boot 'em out, only it ain't their fault. They're both the same. Their 'eads is like leaky tins. Yer can push in as much as yer like but it all comes out again.'

The judge had at last found his voice and from utter stupefaction was becoming interested.

'How did you get them through at all?' he asked.

'Found yer voice, eh? Good. I'll tell yer.   Well, I tole you their two 'eads were like tins with 'oles in 'em. So it's no good trying to fill 'em up. So wot I do is this. I fill 'em up just below the first 'ole, see.'

'How d'you do that?' asked the judge.

'Concentrate on one subject only. That's something. That means they'll get one O and one A at least. Better than none of either. Oh, they won't be eddicated. I can't 'elp that. It's the fault of the system. If I 'ad my way, my boys would learn a good bit less but they'd learn it good. It'd stick and they'd ask for more. That's the way to teach. A level and O level! Pah!'

And he pulled both blinds down sharply, as though to emphasize his disgust.

'Well,' said the judge. 'Thank you for this exposition. First of all, I should like to apologise for not realising who you were.'

'No 'ard feelings, mate,' said the headmaster. 'Shake.' And he held out his hand. The judge shook it.

'How d'you do?' he said.

'Nicely, thanks,' said the headmaster.

'What subjects do you teach personally, may I ask?' said the judge after a short pause.

'I do a bit of each mostly,' said the headmaster. 'Greek, Latin, Maffimatics, Physics and all that stuff.'

'English?' queried the judge.

'No, yer got me there, mate. My English is orl right mind yer, just for ordinary talking. But when it comes to Shakespeare and such I can 'ear myself that there's something missing.'

He then proceeded to recite in violent Cockney several extracts from *Hamlet* and *Macbeth* and finally wound up with the whole of the balcony scene from *Romeo and Juliet*.

'Don't sound so good, do it?' he said.

'You've a remarkable memory,' said the judge in genuine admiration.

'Not bad,' said the headmaster modestly, for the first time speaking in his ordinary voice. The change of voice was almost as great a shock to the judge as the shock of finding that this was the headmaster.

'As a matter of fact,' went on the headmaster, in his

F

normal voice, 'I could give you six books of the Aeneid and the whole of the Iliad if you'd like it. But I mustn't keep you. Did you just want to have a look round or was there something else?'

The judge sat back in his chair. 'Well really!' he said eventually. 'I can hardly be blamed for my mistake. Do you play this game on all your visitors?'

'No,' said the headmaster, 'I choose them most carefully. I've never been called on by a judge before. It was an opportunity I couldn't miss. Please forgive me.'

'Very well,' said the judge. 'If the performance is over, perhaps I can tell you why I've called.'

'Look, chum,' said the headmaster, 'don't come the old acid. It's you wot wants something outer me, ain't it?'

'You're quite right,' said the judge. 'I apologise.'

'O.K., guv,' said the headmaster. 'And now what can I do for you?'

'I'm making enquiries about an old boy of yours. He wasn't here in your time, I imagine. Before the last war, as a matter of fact.'

'I bin 'ere four years come Christmas,' said the headmaster. 'Or I should say I shall have had this appointment four years next Christmas.'

'Please don't exert yourself for me,' said the judge. 'I can understand you very well.'

'Back slang and all?' asked the headmaster.

'I know what it is,' said the judge, 'but I couldn't follow it if you talked quickly.'

'I must admit I'm a bit rusty on that,' said the headmaster.

'Well, if I may get down to business,' said the judge. 'The name is William Burford.'

'Oh, we know all about him. 'E's in the nick, ain't 'e? I should say that——'

'You needn't translate,' said the judge. 'Yes, he's in prison. I sent him there.'

'Breaking into a bank or something. Well, it's better

than picking pockets. Must take some guts. All the same, we don't actually teach it here. Well, what can I tell you about him?'

'To tell you the truth,' said the judge, 'I don't really know. But, since the case has been over, I've taken an interest in the man and his wife and it's possible I can help them.'

'Well, he doesn't come back to the school,' said the headmaster, 'and, from what I read, he isn't likely to for some time. But I'll send for his record. We try to keep up with all the old boys.'

He pressed a bell and shortly afterwards there was a knock at the door. The headmaster's secretary came in. She was an efficient-looking middle-aged woman.

'We've an enquiry for an old boy. Can you bring his record, please, Pimple?'

'The confidential one, sir?' said Miss Pimple in an ultra refined voice.

'Under our system,' the headmaster explained, 'we keep two cards. One we can show to anyone and one with the truth, what he was like at school, who his friends were and so on.'

'It would be most helpful if I could see the confidential card,' said the judge. 'I should particularly like to know who his friends were.'

'Right,' said the headmaster. 'We've a customer, Pimple, let's hope the system works.'

'And the name, sir?' said Miss Pimple. 'The system would not work without a name.'

'Wot's in a name?' said the headmaster. 'No, you say it, Pimple,' he added. 'Sounds better from you.'

'That,' said Miss Pimple, 'which we call a rose by any other name would smell as sweet. And the name is, sir?'

'William Burford,' said the judge. 'I should imagine that he was here between 1934 and 1939. Something like that.'

'Thank you, sir,' said Miss Pimple. 'I'll get it at once.'

' "Stand not upon the order of your going," ' began the headmaster. 'There I am, off again.'

Miss Pimple left, and the judge continued his chat with the headmaster. He decided to take full advantage of meeting this remarkable man.

'To what do you attribute the present increase in crime?' he said.

'Keeps you busy, doesn't it?' said the headmaster. 'Lack of education in the right subjects mostly. I might have been a burglar or something for all the education I had. It's all this O level, A level and eleven-plus. First you've got to teach the parents. Then you won't have to teach the sons and daughters. But who is teaching the parents? Here I have four hundred and thirty-two future parents and how many hours a week can I teach them the things that really matter? Two. Two flippin' hours a week, that's all. I beg your pardon. Two solitary hours. Mind you, that's better than most places where they don't have it for two flippin'—two solitary—minutes. I'm not saying knowledge is a bad thing. On the contrary. But no amount of knowledge is any good wivout you understand wot you've got to do wiv it, that is to say—but you understand, I see. Well, I take every boy in this school on How to Live. If they don't learn that, all the Shakespeares and Homers and binomial theorems won't do them any good.'

'How do you teach them to live, may I ask?' said the judge.

'By example, mostly. "'Ere, Spriggs," I say, "you're a married man with two children and you meet a beautiful girl in your office wot gives yer the orl right signal." That's for the older boys, of course. But similar with the younger ones. Cheating the railways, and so on. Oh no, it isn't a lot of pi jaw. It's business, that's what it is. Here, I'll show you. I'll turn on Smith minor.'

He went to a tape recorder and set it going at the place he wanted. The judge immediately heard the voice of the headmaster talking to a small boy.

'Now, Smith, what is meant by telling the truth?'

'Not telling lies.'

'Why not tell lies?'

'Because it doesn't pay.'

'Why doesn't it pay?'

'Because no one would ever trust you.'

There was a noise at the door and Miss Pimple came in with two cards.

'Thank you, Pimple,' said the headmaster.

'I'll have ready the cards of this boy's friends, sir.'

'I'll ring twice if I want them, Pimple, thanks ever so,' said the headmaster, and Miss Pimple went out without the trace of a smile. She was obviously used to the headmaster's little ways and she simply ignored them. Oxford or Bermondsey was all the same to her.

They looked at the cards.

'This is the chap all right,' said the judge looking at one of the cards. 'Married Lesley Elizabeth Rogers, September 1950.'

'This is the one you want,' said the headmaster. 'Six months for receiving, February 1947. Now let's see him at school.'

The headmaster looked at the card. 'Not a bad chap really. Rather easily led. Weak character: all right in the right company.'

'Had he a friend called Wilson?'

'What initials?'

'C. M.'

'Yes he had. This will interest you. This fellow Wilson was a gambler, borrowed money and didn't pay it back. Not enough proved to expel. Bad influence on Burford. We'd better send for Master Wilson's card.'

He rang the bell twice and after a very short while Miss Pimple appeared with several cards.

'Confidential on C. M. Wilson, please, Pimple.'

'I opined you'd want him, sir. It's at the top.'

She brought out the card.

'Do you wish any of the others, sir?'

'Leave them with us, Pimple, please.'

Miss Pimple put down the cards. 'Anything else before I go for my beer, sir?' she said.

'No thanks, Pimple. Keep half a pint for me.'

'Very good, sir. Mild or bitter?'

'The usual, Pimple, please.'

Miss Pimple went out.

'Irreplaceable,' said the headmaster. 'Lots can do shorthand and typing and the rest. But how many can take their beer?'

'This man Wilson,' said the judge, 'his Christian names are?'

'Cedric Mattingly.'

'That's the man,' said the judge. 'I knew there was something in it. But why on earth didn't they want to say that he was at school with him? I suppose he's got some convictions against him, or something.'

The headmaster suddenly looked more serious.

'He might have, if he'd lived, poor chap,' he said, 'but he's dead, killed in the war. Paid his debts all right.'

'Dead, did you say?' asked the judge.

'Yes, killed in action in the desert—1943. It's funny, you know. He was a bad hat all right, judging from his report. But because he was killed, we wipe it all out. He may have been called up and been a bad soldier. But he was killed. And that balances the lot. Oh well, I suppose it's right. Life's the thing we all want most, and Cedric Mattingly Wilson hasn't got his any more. We've got ours, though.'

'And his full name again?'

'Cedric Mattingly Wilson.'

'There can't be two people of that name. Wilson's common enough but there couldn't be more than one Cedric Mattingly Wilson.'

'There aren't any of him now, poor fellow,' said the headmaster.

'I wouldn't have believed it,' said the judge. 'And yet somehow I knew.'

'What is it? You seem to have had a shock. What about a glass of beer? It's gone eleven.'

'No, thank you,' said the judge. 'Yes, indeed, I have had a shock. I may tell you, Mr Sprout, that I have been going up and down England looking for this man Wilson.'

'That's hard,' said the headmaster. 'He couldn't very well be here. You couldn't call England heaven or hell. Purgatory, perhaps, though.'

'I'm afraid I don't find it a joke,' said the judge.

'No, I'm sorry. But have you really been looking for a dead man?'

'Yes,' said the judge, 'I have.'

'Who told you he was alive?'

'Burford and his wife.'

'They did, did they? Well, they picked the wrong man to say that to.'

'I'm not sure that they did, Mr Sprout. Because I believed them. Do you know that that woman has actually sent for me twice because she has said she had the man under observation?'

'What for?'

'You may well ask. It's one of two motives. Either to get money out of me—and she has, a little—or to revenge herself on me for sending her husband to prison.'

'In other words, mate, you've been 'ad for a sucker?'

'Yes,' said the judge. 'That's exactly what has happened. When I think what I've done to try to help her find Wilson—they said he was going under the name of Thompson, but that his real name was Wilson, Cedric Mattingly Wilson—when I think of all she's persuaded me to do, I feel—well, to tell you the truth, Mr Sprout, I hardly know how I do feel. All the time I've felt there was something else about the case, and she's even told me lies which she's later admitted were lies. And then each time she's persuaded me that there were reasons for her lies and that the substantial truth lay on her side.'

'What has Wilson got to do with it? Why do you want to find him?'

'He's supposed to be the man who committed the crime for which her husband went to prison.'

'Well, he can't have, can he?'

'No,' said the judge, 'he can't.'

'What are you going to do about it?'

'I must think it out,' said the judge, 'but I think I ought to prosecute her.'

'I should hope so. We can't have judges being made more fools of than they—we can't have judges being made fools of, can we?'

The judge was so used to Mr Sprout by now and so entirely devoted in his mind to his appalling discovery that the sally passed unnoticed.

'I confess I don't like the idea of the publicity,' he said, 'but I can't really see any alternative. I shall go and consult the Director of Public Prosecutions immediately. Thank you very much for your help.'

'Glad to have been of help but sorry it's been such a knockout.'

He led the judge from the room towards the entrance. They passed the War Memorial. The judge looked at it and with unpleasant fascination saw in its expected place among those killed in the 1939-45 War, Private Cedric Mattingly Wilson.

CHAPTER TWENTY-TWO

A Plain Case of Fraud

THE next day the judge interviewed the Director of Public Prosecutions and disclosed the main facts to him.

'Undoubtedly,' he said, 'I've made a fool of myself and it will appear so to the public, but all the same I personally think the public interest requires that the woman should be prosecuted.'

'Presumably for obtaining money by false pretences,' said the Director.

'Yes,' said the judge. 'All the ingredients are there. One way or another she's had about £150 out of me. Whether, strictly speaking, the money I paid direct to the detective could be made the subject of a charge, I'm not sure. I should think not. But the money she got for paying the man she said was her informant certainly can. I don't suppose for a moment that he exists. But, even if he did, she got the money from me to pay him by pretending Thompson was alive when she knew he wasn't.'

'But how can her informant exist?' queried the Director. 'She knew the man was dead. So she couldn't possibly have asked someone to find him.'

'I agree,' said the judge, 'that must be right. But there's no point in putting that in the charge. We've got a straightforward pretence that Thompson was alive.'

'Oh, certainly,' said the Director. 'There's just one thing and, as far as I can see, only one. I know it's in the highest degree unlikely—particularly having regard to the reluctance of both Burfords to admit that the boys were at school together—but theoretically, I suppose, there could be two Cedric Mattingly Wilsons. The coincidences would be incredible but I think we've got to stop up that hole before we proceed.'

'How do you suggest doing so?'

'If you don't mind, Judge, I would like you to go with a police officer and interview the lady. You can state in her presence what has happened and she can be asked under caution whether she says it is another man and that it is pure coincidence that her husband was at school with someone of exactly the same name with whom he apparently consorted a good deal. If she admits it's the same person or refuses to answer we can go ahead, because we'll know for certain that it is the same person. In the unlikely event of her saying that there is another person the officer must get as much information as he can from her and we must then see if the evidence is sufficient. I shall be very surprised if she tries that, though.'

'I shall not be surprised at anything,' said the judge. 'After the way that woman has pleaded with me on—on—' He was about to say 'on bended knee,' when he suddenly realised that she had done so on his bed and he saw no reason why he should make a present of that to the Director. 'After the way she has pleaded with me to believe her and assured me that Thompson had only gone away a short time before I arrived—and twice, mind you —I'd believe her capable of anything.'

'Well, you'd like to go ahead, Judge, then?'

'Yes, I'm afraid so,' said the judge. 'It'll be great fun for the public and most unpleasant for me, but I think it's my duty.'

He thought for a moment and then added:

'Yes, I can see no alternative.'

'Very well, Judge, I'll arrange for a superintendent to call for you and take you to see the lady. I'll tell him to come and see you first to be briefed and then you can arrange any time that's convenient to you.'

The judge thanked the Director and walked home from his office. It was only on the way home that a horrible thought struck him. He was kicking himself for being such a fool when he remembered Dalmunzie's warning, 'Lock your bedroom door.' It pulled him up short in his thoughts. This woman was plainly a dangerous woman. Her exact object might never be known, but she was prepared to lie her head off. He had, in fact, behaved with perfect propriety when she came to his bedroom but whose word was there for that except his? If she alleged that they were lovers and, for example, that the Thompson business was just a fiction between them to cover up their relationship and that he only prosecuted her when she refused to comply with his abnormal sexual demands!

They were horrifying thoughts. It was not that his friends would disbelieve him but at the best, even if the woman's story were not entirely credited, some members of the public would feel that there was something in it. And then another terrible thought struck him. Suppose Burford petitioned for divorce on the ground of her adultery with him. Again, his friends would believe him and in view of her lies about Thompson, most of the public would believe him too, but some might not. And then, again, who was to prove the lies except himself?

Mr Maclachlan, she can say, was just part of the scheme, in case her husband found out. And, after all, he would have to admit that he, a High Court Judge, had attended six race-meetings with the woman and stayed the night in the same hotel. He would also have to admit that she had come to his bedroom in her nightclothes while he was in bed and thrown herself in his arms.

'Oh, my God!' he said to himself. He had done nothing wrong and everything from a good motive, and yet it was not absolutely impossible that not only would the woman be acquitted but he himself found guilty of adultery. And, of adultery in the worst possible circumstances—with the wife of a man he had sent to prison. He had done things which can never have been done before and, from the public's point of view, if a judge—a widower—did such very odd things, was it so unlikely that he would also do a very natural thing and sleep with an exceptionally attractive woman?

He could now see himself completely ruined by the affair. Why on earth had he embarked on it? Well, it was no good thinking about that. The question was, what was he to do now? Just nothing? Perhaps that was the best solution. But, then, suppose the woman did try to blackmail him or suppose divorce proceedings were brought against him, he would have to explain the delay in taking action after he first learned the truth about Thompson. What answer could he give except that he was frightened of the consequences? That was the truth. But why frightened if he had done nothing wrong? How could he successfully explain to a judge or jury or the public the motives which prevented him taking action with a certainty of being believed? If he had not done such extraordinary things in the first instance the matter would have been very different.

By the time he reached home he was drenched with sweat. He had a bath and changed and thought about the matter again. He called up his resources on the other side. He had an absolutely clear conscience, he had acted solely to see if an injustice had been done. His reputation was of the highest. It was surely very odd that such a judge should suddenly stoop to behave in such a scandalous manner. And he could certainly prove that he had tried to get the man off and out of prison. That was quite inconsistent with adultery.

Then he became angry with himself. Here he was almost hounding himself out of society, when he it was who had been the victim. He was the wronged person. Why should he be so frightened?

And then the forces of fear came into play again. What about the woman who committed suicide when the charge of rape she had made was dismissed? May she not have had a clear conscience and been unable to stand the verdict of acquittal which reflected guilt on her? Everyone is nearly always on the side of the person in the dock. He gets all the sympathy. They don't think of the chief witness for the prosecution whose reputation may be gravely damaged by an acquittal, with no possibility of redress.

Then he fought back again and the first weapon he used was his recollection of Lesley's face. She did not look like a blackmailer. She undoubtedly had a very sweet face. Surely she couldn't be capable of doing what he was imagining. And yet she was capable of the most genuine looking tears and protestations of telling the truth when in fact the whole thing was a pack of lies from beginning to end.

After a pause in the battle he pulled himself together. He must decide what he was to do. Cry the whole thing off or prosecute? He came to a decision for two reasons. First, he was in the right and he would not yield to the forces of wrong, whatever the consequences; and, secondly, if he did nothing, he would never know whether the woman was going to make allegations against him. He was not prepared to wonder about this. She would have to make her allegations almost immediately if they were to be believed. Indeed, perhaps it would be as well if in the presence of the superintendent he recited what had happened at the hotel. Not as though he were defending himself at all, but, on the contrary, as evidence against the woman of the lengths she went to deceive him.

He made up his mind only just in time, as the superintendent telephoned and asked when it would be convenient for him to call and have a chat about the matter.

CHAPTER TWENTY-THREE

The Problem

THE superintendent was punctual for his appointment and they proceeded to discuss the case immediately. The judge told him everything except that Lesley's final plea at Doncaster had been in the bedroom. He was to regret not having mentioned this almost immediately. When he had finished his story, punctuated by a few questions from the superintendent, the judge asked him if there was anything more he would like to know. The superintendent thought for a moment and then coughed before asking his first question. The slight cough before starting a cross-examination is a normal sign of nervousness in an advocate and the superintendent's cough had the same significance.

'Sir Gerald,' he said, 'this woman, we know, is a consummate liar. She may be dangerous too. It's important that I should know in advance if possible, what truth, if any, there is in what she says.'

He stopped and the judge said in perhaps a slightly testy voice, which did not lessen the Superintendent's nervousness:

'Well, what else is there that you want to know?'

The superintendent coughed again. The judge noticed it and was not pleased.

'Have you a sore throat, Superintendent?' he asked. 'If so, I can provide you with a lozenge.'

The superintendent, after a moment's thought, decided to accept the invitation. The conversation was, therefore, slightly delayed while the judge fetched a box of lozenges.

'Thank you, sir,' said the superintendent, 'it is most kind.'

'Not at all,' said the judge. 'Now we can get on. You were saying something.'

'It was just this.' The superintendent just managed to repress a cough and took a vigorous suck at the lozenge instead. The judge winced. It was a sound he could not bear, and he regretted his impetuosity in offering the lozenges. He knew from experience that the awful noise would continue through their conversation. Noisy eaters and sweet suckers who take an audible suck at least once every half minute were two of his abominations. There was an awful fascination about it too, like water dripping at long intervals from a tap. You never knew when the next suck was coming.

'You might find it rather too strong, Superintendent,' said the judge hopefully. 'If you'd like to get rid of it, please do. Here's an ashtray.'

'No, indeed, thank you, Sir Gerald,' said the superintendent. 'I like it very much. It's more like a sweet really,' and he took a vigorous suck.

'Might I perhaps know what they're called?' he added.

'The name's on the tin,' said the judge and pushed it rather grudgingly across the table.

'*Succaroles*,' read the superintendent. 'I've never heard of them before. I must remember the name.'

And he sucked again.

'Now,' said the judge, 'perhaps . . .' and he waited for the superintendent's question.

'It's just this, Sir Gerald. There may have been trifling things which you haven't thought worth mentioning. Names, for example.'

'What do you mean?' said the judge.

'Well, I don't want to alarm you, Sir Gerald, but we may be dealing with rather desperate people. And they're certainly quite unscrupulous.'

'I quite follow that,' said the judge, 'but I wish you

wouldn't beat about the bush. Ask me in plain English what you want to know about names.'

'Well, Sir Gerald, what used you to call her?'

'Call her? By her name, of course, Mrs Burford.'

'You never used her Christian name?'

'No, certainly not.'

'I'm sorry to annoy you, Sir Gerald, but . . .'

'You're not annoying me in the least,' said the judge angrily. 'Kindly ask any further questions you wish.'

'You see, Sir Gerald, supposing, when we went in, she greeted you by your Christian name, I should know, as you weren't on Christian name terms, what she was up to.'

'What would she be up to?'

'Well, Sir Gerald, I've had pretty good experience of this sort of woman. Even if she isn't a blackmailer by profession, with her back against the wall she may try anything. Now, if you had been on Christian name terms, the mere fact that she called you by your Christian name wouldn't mean anything. As it is, it will be an immediate danger signal and we'll know the sort of thing to expect.'

'Such as, Superintendent?'

'Oh, anything. Forgive me putting it this way, Sir Gerald, but she might allege anything—absolutely anything.'

'Do explain, Superintendent. What do you mean by anything?'

'Well, Sir Gerald, we're men of the world and you'll forgive this, I'm sure, but if it starts off that way she might allege—she might suggest—she might imply or actually say—she might treat your relationship with her as though . . . as though . . .'

'As though we'd slept together. If that's what you mean, Superintendent, for Heaven's sake say so.'

'Well, of course, it would be incorrect, but it's the sort of thing those women do. In so many cases it's most difficult to refute, and they know it. It's just word against word and, as men do sleep with women, they hope they may be believed. Of course, in your case, no one would believe it for a moment. You did unfortunately stay in the same hotel together—I don't mean together, of course, but on the same night. But I expect your room was nowhere near hers.'

'I've no idea where it was.'

'Anyway she was never in your room and you were never in hers. She'll lie about that, of course, if she's the sort of woman I'm referring to, but no doubt your word would be accepted. The difficult cases are where the parties have been in the same room and it's just a question of what happened when they were there.'

'As a matter of fact,' said the judge, 'she did come to my room.'

'She came to your room?'

'Yes, I'm afraid so.'

'You hadn't asked her to do so?'

'Of course I hadn't. She came and woke me up in the middle of the night.'

'Oh, I see,' said the superintendent, 'so you weren't both fully dressed.'

'Of course we weren't, Superintendent. I was fully undressed. I was in bed and asleep in my pyjamas.'

'And she?'

'She was in pyjamas and a dressing-gown.'

'I'm afraid this looks serious, Sir Gerald. This looks like the real thing. It's an old game. Did . . . er . . . er . . . anything take place between you?'

'Of course something took place between us,' said the judge angrily.

The superintendent gaped.

'If you didn't waltz around the matter, Superintendent, we'd get on quicker. If you were woken up in the middle of the night by a woman, she wouldn't just stand there saying nothing and you wouldn't lie there doing nothing. Something would happen, wouldn't it? If it was only that you told her to get out, as I did.'

G

'Is the woman . . . er . . . good looking at all?'

'Yes, she is . . . very,' said the judge.

'I see,' said the superintendent. 'And all that happened was that you told her to go and she went.'

'No,' said the judge, 'I told her to go and she didn't.'

'So you rang the bell and had her turned out?'

'No,' said the judge, 'I didn't. I threatened to and she pleaded with me to go on helping.'

'She didn't by any chance throw her arms round you while she was pleading with you?'

'Well, she did, as a matter of fact.'

The superintendent thought for a moment.

'This is going to be extremely awkward, Sir Gerald. This looks to me pretty well like a typical case. These women are the very devil. They'll allege anything, and particularly with someone in your position. She'll know that you won't want the publicity. And she may do it out of pure vindictiveness, even if she's got nothing to gain by it for herself.'

'What are you leading up to, Superintendent?'

'Well, sir, she may not be a blackmailer in the first instance. Some of these women who get money by fraud simply keep this sort of thing as an avenue of escape. In other words, they won't blackmail you for money, but, if a prosecution is threatened, they'll try and head it off by threats of this kind, and, if you call their bluff and prosecute, they make good their threats out of pure spite.'

'I still ask you, Superintendent, what all this is leading up to.'

It was no comfort to the judge that the superintendent was saying what had been thought of by him the day before. He was indeed horrified to find how right he was.

'I was only wondering, Sir Gerald, if in the circumstances you wanted to prosecute.'

'I've discussed the matter with the Director and we've decided that it's the only proper course.'

'Then the Director knows all you've told me, Sir Gerald?'

'Not quite,' said the judge a little uncomfortably. 'I didn't mention the bedroom scene. It didn't seem to be relevant at the time. But I do now see its importance.'

'It looks so premeditated, Sir Gerald. That's what troubles me.'

'But, if she's going to try blackmail, surely she'd have started by now.'

'Not necessarily, Sir Gerald. And anyway, as I said, she may not intend to use blackmail except as a defence.'

'Well, I don't see how I can leave the matter as it is,' said the judge. 'This woman has obtained money from me by blatant persistent fraud. I have, in fact, done absolutely nothing wrong. I have simply, no doubt unwisely, been rather foolish in letting myself get into this position. In those circumstances it seems to me that it would not only be cowardly but contrary to my duty as a judge if I let the matter go, just because I am frightened of the possible consequences to myself. One might just as well have a bachelor High Court Judge refusing to prosecute a burglar because it was suspected that entirely false allegations would be made by the burglar. In my view I'm under a duty to prosecute or rather to set the wheels of prosecution in motion. Of course the Director will prosecute. I shall simply be the chief witness. Besides,' he added, 'there's always the possibility that she is a blackmailer, and would have to be prosecuted for that later. If that happened, the failure to prosecute now would make it look as if I had something to hide, and lend colour to the allegations she would no doubt make on her prosecution.'

'I see your point, Sir Gerald. And also, of course, you would always have it hanging over your head, and you may prefer to know the worst now rather than wait for it.'

The judge did not at all relish the way in which the superintendent was voicing his doubts of the day before.

He had hoped that he had allowed his imagination and anxiety too much play, but here was a down-to-earth superintendent, who probably hadn't much imagination, saying almost exactly the same as he had thought. All the same, he could see no escape from it. There must be a prosecution. He said so to the superintendent.

'Very good, Sir Gerald. We'll go and see the lady. I suggest we don't give her any warning. Usually I find early in the morning say, nine o'clock, is a good time to find these ladies in. If that isn't too early for you, Sir Gerald.'

'No, that will be all right.'

'I'll call for you then, Sir Gerald, at 8.45 a.m.'

'Thank you. That will be very helpful.'

The superintendent got up.

'Well,' he said, 'let's hope things won't be as bad as we fear, but I'm not very hopeful.'

He started to go.

'Of course, there wasn't anything else, Sir Gerald?'

The judge paused for a moment.

'She kissed me on the forehead, if you must know.'

'But there was no other kissing?'

'*There was not,*' said the judge decisively and rather loudly.

'I'm so sorry to have embarrassed you, Sir Gerald.'

'You have not embarrassed me in the least,' said the judge. 'Good morning. I'll see you tomorrow,' and he let out the superintendent as quickly as he could.

CHAPTER TWENTY-FOUR

Under Caution

THE next day, after a most troubled night, the judge set off with the superintendent, who was in plain clothes, for the house where Lesley had rooms. She was in and opened the front door herself. The judge was ready for the worst fears of the superintendent to be realised, and for her to throw her arms around his neck and call him by unsuitable endearing names. But, when he saw her, he felt relieved. He felt instinctively that anyone who looked like Lesley could not conceivably be a blackmailer. Her sweet face had a tremendous effect on him and he had to remind himself of the outrageous lies she had told, in order to rid himself of his immediate reaction to seeing her again. It was some time since he had last seen her and he had rather forgotten what an appealing face she had. And here he was with the crushing weight of the law beside him about to add to her misery. Then quickly he recalled the number of times she had assured him that she had seen Thompson and her appearance of honesty as she said it. You simply cannot judge by a face, he said to himself. The sweetest most appealing face in the world may conceal the mind of a completely unscrupulous adventurer.

'May we come in?' he said.

'Of course,' said Lesley. 'Please do.'

They went into her sitting room.

'This is Superintendent Neale of Scotland Yard,' said the judge.

They both waited for her reaction. It was not what they

had expected. Her face lighted up and she said excitedly:
'Have you found him then? How wonderful.'

The superintendent, though a little surprised at her behaviour, said nothing but grimly admired her performance. What an actress the woman is, he thought. She almost deserves to get away with it. And, by Jove! the judge was right when he said she was attractive. I know what my wife would say to me if she came into my bedroom in her nightclothes. His wife had not much imagination, but, he reflected, she would not require to draw very much on her small store of it to say what she thought of that situation.

No one answered Lesley immediately, and, when she saw how serious they looked, her face fell.

'Has something happened to William?' she asked anxiously. 'Has he escaped again? I begged him not to try.'

'No,' said the judge, 'he hasn't escaped.'

Again there was silence. Then Lesley began again but rather less brightly:

'Then it is about him—Thompson, I mean?'

'Yes,' said the judge unsmiling. 'It is about him.'

She could tell from the way he spoke that it was not good news.

'Has he gone abroad?' she asked. 'Is that it?'

She's a sticker, thought the superintendent. But for brazenness she takes a lot of beating.

'Mrs Burford,' said the judge slowly, 'what do you say Thompson's real or former name was?'

'Cedric Mattingly Wilson,' said Lesley, and started to brighten again.

'Then you have found him?' she said.

Wonderful, thought the superintendent. Like a captain going down with his ship. It's almost pathetic.

'Mrs Burford,' said the judge. 'A few days ago I went to see the headmaster of your husband's school.'

Lesley went white. She was standing and the super-

intendent thought she might be going to faint. So he
steadied her with his arm.

'No, it's all right,' she said and sat down in a chair.
'Just let me think for a moment.'

The judge was so relieved at Lesley's behaviour that he
could only feel sympathy for her. All his own fears
vanished in a moment, and all he could see was a pathetic
creature, already sufficiently unhappy, about to be made
even more so. Then he realised that his fears might have
been allayed too easily. She hadn't said anything for the
moment. It's true that there had been none of the actions
suggested by the superintendent, but she still might be
thinking out a good lie to tell. After all, she was highly
skilled in the art. No, it was too soon to be sure that he was
safe.

They both waited for her to make the next move. It was
at least a minute before she spoke.

'He's not really dead, you know,' she said.

Really, said the superintendent to himself, this is
carrying things a bit too far. Or she may be out of her
mind. That's possible. However, the first thing to establish
for certain was that there were not two Cedric Mattingly
Wilsons. But it had better be under caution.

'Mrs Burford,' he said, 'I think I should now warn you
that you needn't say anything unless you wish to do so but
that anything you do say may be given in evidence if you
are charged with an offence.'

'What offence?' asked Lesley.

'Obtaining money by false pretences from Sir Gerald
Carstairs.'

'What false pretences?'

I'm losing sympathy with this client, thought the
superintendent. Innocent baby looks and all.

'By falsely pretending that Cedric Mattingly Wilson
was alive when in fact you knew him to be dead.'

'He's alive,' said Lesley.

'Really, Mrs Burford,' said the superintendent. 'Sir

Gerald has seen his name on the Roll of Honour at the School. Are you suggesting that you were referring to a different Cedric Mattingly Wilson?'

'No, that's the one,' said Lesley.

'Well, why do you keep up such a silly pretence?' said the superintendent. 'It'll do you no good. I'm about to go to the War Office for confirmation of his death, but that's only a formality.'

'I know,' said Lesley. 'They'll confirm it.'

'Well,' said the superintendent, 'as I told you, you needn't answer any questions if you prefer not, but is it not the case that you have frequently told Sir Gerald that this man Wilson is alive and that you have obtained money on the strength of it?'

'Yes,' said Lesley, 'that's quite true. Are you arresting me now?'

'No,' said the judge and added very gently, 'but I'm afraid that must follow.'

'I did ask you not to go to the school,' said Lesley.

The superintendent had now got his bearings. These women had two well-known methods of defence. The one was the hell-cat, scratching, fighting, no holds barred method which he had feared. The other was the poor, helpless, innocent, didn't-really-mean-any-harm method, which this girl was putting on to a treat. Now *his* only fear was that the judge would be taken in by it and call off the prosecution, not through fear but through pity. He was glad it was that way, as the other would have been more embarrassing, but, all the same, he wasn't going to let this bird get away, if he could help it.

'Now, Mrs Burford,' he said, 'I propose to write out what you have said and ask you if you will sign it. You needn't if you don't wish to do so.'

'I'll sign it,' she said. 'Will I go to prison for long?'

'It's possible,' said the judge, 'only possible, mind you, that you won't go to prison at all. It's the first offence, you see.'

'It isn't an offence at all,' said Lesley, 'but you'll never believe me. The man is alive.'

'Now, look, Mrs Burford,' said the superintendent, quite sincerely, 'what the judge has said is quite true and with luck you won't be sent to prison. I'd like to help you but you make it very difficult for us if you keep on telling lies about this man. We all know he's dead now. Why keep up the pretence?'

'It's not a pretence,' said Lesley.

'But the War Office can prove he's dead. What's the good of saying he's still alive? The War Office don't make mistakes like that. Not once in a thousand years.'

'Then this is the thousandth year,' said Lesley.

'Mrs Burford,' said the judge, 'are you feeling quite well?'

'I'm feeling sick,' said Lesley, 'but I'm quite well really.'

'Why do you keep repeating this nonsense about the man being alive?'

'Because I've seen him. Haven't I told you? Twice I've seen him.'

'But he's dead.'

'He isn't.'

'Can you explain then how he's officially reported dead?'

'Well, I can but I don't suppose you'll believe me.'

'What is the explanation?'

'This man Thompson or Wilson came to see my husband shortly before the robbery. They were at school together, but they hadn't met each other for years.'

'Why did you lie about their being at school together?'

'That's easy. I'll tell you. When the police first called on William he was a little anxious about what he'd been doing with Thompson on race-courses, but that was all. But later, when they identified the notes and the dust and he realised that no one believed his story about Thompson, he was terrified to say they were at school together.

Just as later on I was. In case you went there and found
he was dead. He felt it would be the final nail in *his* coffin.
And we lied. I'm right about that, aren't I? William's
case would have been more difficult at the trial if Thompson were proved to be dead.'

'Well, of course. Then he is dead?'

'No, I tell you, he isn't, but who would have believed
us? You won't believe me now. But I'd better tell you just
the same. Shall I?'

'If it's the truth,' said the judge. 'But don't, if it isn't.'

'You won't believe it, but it is the truth,' said Lesley.
'When Thompson first called on us, William was amazed,
as he'd heard he'd been killed. "I was," said Thompson,
"or rather Cedric Mattingly Wilson was killed. My
name's Thompson. It was too easy, really," he said. "I
owed a lot all round and for various reasons it would have
suited me well to disappear. I got my chance in the
desert. Found a dead private and put my identity disc on
him. Then deserted and got taken prisoner. I escaped and
one way or another I managed to get home to start a new
life as Thompson. I got ration cards and everything.
Thompson's the name now," he said.'

'That's all very well,' said the judge. 'But first of all,
this is a very old story and not at all easy to bring off. It
has no doubt very occasionally happened but it's not so
simple as you think. But, if this man did say all this, you
knew I was trying to help you, why didn't you tell
me?'

'*Because* you were helping me. You were my only hope.
If you stopped helping me, there was nothing more I
could do. And I felt sure that, if I told you the story about
Thompson, you'd make enquiries at the War Office and
find he was dead and disbelieve me. You don't believe me
now, do you?'

The superintendent looked at the judge to see who
should say 'No' first.

'I'm afraid not,' said the judge. 'You have unfortun-

ately told me other lies and I'm afraid I can't accept what
you say now.'

'I didn't expect you to,' said Lesley. 'That's why I
didn't tell you before. Can't you see that?'

'I hear what you say,' said the judge.

'And why should I have done all I have, unless Thompson did exist? What good have I got out of it?'

'You've had fifty pounds,' said the superintendent,
'apart from some visits to race-courses and meals at Sir
Gerald's expense.'

'The fifty pounds were for the man who answered the
advertisement.'

'So you say,' said the superintendent, 'can you prove
he exists?'

'I don't know,' said Lesley, 'but that sort of man isn't
very free with his address.'

'Well, then,' said the superintendent, 'from my point of
view the answer to your question is £50 and any more you
might have been able to get out of Sir Gerald.'

'Do you think that too?' Lesley asked the judge.

'What else can I think?' he said. 'You lied to me on at
least two occasions and now you expect us to believe a
fantastic story which, if true, your husband could have
told at his trial as you could have told me.'

'But I've explained why we both didn't. I dare say it
was wrong but then the odds were so much against us. I
don't know what else we could have done. You've
admitted that William would have been even more sure
to have been convicted, and by your own behaviour now
I can see I was right not to tell you, or you'd have stopped
helping me at once. Not that it would have made any
difference,' she added. 'I am really grateful for your help,'
she said, 'but all it's done, so far as I can see, is to land me
in the dock. Not that I care much. With William in prison,
I might as well be. Only it's so unjust. We have been
foolish and told lies, but they weren't crimes. Now he's
doing ten years for something he never did and I'm about

to be prosecuted for something I never did. Now if I told a lie now and said Thompson really was dead, you'd tell me it would help me not to go to prison. Well, I'm not going to, even if it does mean prison. He's alive and I shall say so. Doesn't that make you think I may be telling the truth?'

'A very good effort, Mrs Burford,' said the judge. 'It's a pity you don't use your obvious talents for a better purpose.'

'I can hear you saying that from the Bench with a sneer,' said Lesley. 'Go on, prosecute me. But I shall tell the truth and the whole truth this time.'

The *whole* truth, thought the superintendent. Were my first thoughts right? Has she tried the little girl stuff first and is she now going to try the other? Well, fortunately for the judge, she won't get very far with it now. She should have started off with that one if she wanted it to work. All the same she can make a lot of the bedroom scene if she wants to be nasty. Yes, of course, he thought, and she can say she didn't want to say anything about it, unless it was absolutely necessary. Yes, we mustn't be too confident.

Meanwhile the judge's thoughts were running on the same lines, and he felt that it was advisable to say:

'Yes, Mrs Burford, I should tell the whole truth if I were you. And, if there's anything you've left out that you'd like to tell the superintendent I suggest you do so now, though, of course, you needn't if you don't want to. But, if you bring out some further bombshell at a later date, you mustn't be surprised if people aren't inclined to believe you. You've a chance of saying it now, you see.'

Cunning old boy, thought the superintendent, couldn't have done it better myself. If she says nothing about the bedroom now, she won't get much out of it later.

'No,' said Lesley, 'I can't think of anything else. Thompson planted everything on William and he's alive. And that's all there is to it.'

The judge and the superintendent left Lesley a few minutes after the superintendent had put her statement into writing and she had signed it.

'Well, Sir Gerald,' said the superintendent on their way to the judge's flat, 'I think we can say that was pretty satisfactory.'

'Yes,' said the judge, 'I think it was. It doesn't look as though there is any thought in her mind of attacking me. I must say, though, I find the way she sticks to her story odd.'

'Oh, Sir Gerald,' said the superintendent, 'you wouldn't if you'd had my experience. Some of these people simply can't give in. All the facts are against them but they still brazen it out.'

'And what has she to gain from it?'

'Nothing,' said the superintendent, 'nor have any of the people I have just mentioned, but they do it just the same. Well, I'll get on to the War Office straight away and report the whole matter to the Director. It's pretty well open and shut, I should say. That old identity-disc-from-a-dead-soldier yarn won't last her very long. But I'm sorry in a way, because it might land her in prison. Still, you can't say we didn't give her every chance.'

CHAPTER TWENTY-FIVE

Extraordinary

AFTER the interview with Lesley the judge was as convinced of her guilt as he was before. Indeed, in some ways, he would have had more respect for Lesley, if she had not tried to impose upon them with the well-worn story of the man who puts his identity disc on a dead man. It was an insult to their intelligence. He was quite certain, as was the superintendent, that nothing of the kind had happened. And both of them were, of course, quite right. Cedric Mattingly Wilson had never done such a thing or thought of doing it.

But the judge was greatly relieved by Lesley's attitude and he then began to think of her with both pity and gratitude. After all, she might have done the things which he and the superintendent had visualised. She had tried none of them. It is true that she had attempted to get out of her impossible position by persisting in a stupid lie but that was far, far better than the method of defence he had feared she might use.

Having got to that stage, he began to ask why she had done any of the things she had done. Was it really to make money out of him? If so, she had made very poor use of her chances. Never throughout their association had she mentioned her own financial position, except when the question of paying the informant arose. It was true that very probably that was just a trick and there was no informant. But it was very odd that that was all she had done.

If her object was revenge, she had had every opportunity after the bedroom scene to give effect to any such motive, but she plainly had no such intention.

Eventually the only solution he could arrive at was that she was intending to get more money from him later. He could not pretend that he thought this was an entirely satisfactory solution but, of course, criminals went about their work in an odd way, sometimes making the most stupid mistakes and sometimes taking a great deal of trouble for no good purpose. Yes, that was really the answer. After all, the facts one could not get away from were first that Thompson was to her knowledge dead and secondly that she had pretended he was alive. No, he decided, she was just an odd girl who went about her business in an odd way. It was a pity she had such a sweet, appealing face, but, he supposed, hers would not be the first sweet appealing face in the dock and unquestionably she must go there.

Two days later the telephone rang and the superintendent asked if he could come to see him immediately. Something extraordinary had happened. The judge invited him to call at once.

Something extraordinary? What could it be? Had Lesley turned round and started the course they'd feared? He suddenly felt sick at the thought. After the relief of the last two days he felt he couldn't stand any more of that. But then the word 'extraordinary' didn't suggest that at all. If that is what the superintendent had meant he would have used another expression. He would have said 'I'm afraid something rather unfortunate has happened' or something like that. No, 'extraordinary' wasn't at all the word to use. It was ridiculous of him even to have suspected that Lesley was on the offensive. 'Extraordinary.' Oh, no, that wasn't at all the right word. But then, of course, policemen didn't always have a perfect command of English, and, though the superintendent was reasonably well educated, he had probably risen from the ranks and had a limited vocabulary.

Could he have used the word 'extraordinary' for

'unfortunate,' though? Surely not. He certainly hadn't misheard him. He had definitely said 'something rather extraordinary has happened.' How stupid he was not just to ask one question to relieve his mind of worry. He could so easily have said: 'She hasn't started anything, has she?' or something of that kind. The superintendent could just as easily have allayed his fears on that subject in two words. Why didn't he? Why did he give himself this extra period of uncertainty and suspense?

Well, it wouldn't be for long. It couldn't take the superintendent more than a quarter of an hour to get to him. Of course, if the traffic were bad, it might be longer. Or, if any of the roads were closed for some procession. Thank Heaven, there was nothing on like Trooping the Colour. He looked in *The Times* to see the diary of the day's events. No, there didn't seem to be anything which need delay the superintendent. It was a dry day, too. Of course London traffic did sometimes get out of hand and he might get caught in a traffic block.

The telephone rang. He answered eagerly. If it were the superintendent, he would ask the one question which would prevent the period of waiting from being a period of worry too. Yes, it was Scotland Yard. Good.

'This is Detective-Sergeant Harper speaking, sir. The superintendent was a little delayed in leaving, sir, and he asked me to tell you that he had just left.'

'Thank you,' said the judge and replaced the receiver angrily. Confound it! There was nothing he could ask the sergeant, and now he had to trace the superintendent's journey all over again. How would he come? By the Embankment? Oh, this is absurd. He picked up the newspaper and read the whole of the first leading article without taking in a single word. He tried it again with much the same result, though by means of intense concentration he did manage to follow a few sentences. Where would the superintendent be now? These police-drivers were pretty good. But, of course, he couldn't be ringing the alarm bell and would have to take his place with other traffic. But surely he couldn't be long now. How long did it take to read the leading article? He could time it, and then read it over and over again. Yes, he'd read it aloud. He began:

'The Lord Chancellor's statement yesterday that there would soon be more judges and more Courts will be generally welcomed. It is a truism that justice delayed is justice denied but too many people have in recent years had this fact brought unpleasantly to their attention. It is, however, only fair to the Government to point out that the competitive claims upon the building materials and labour available in the country have until now been very great. Homes must, of course, have first priority, and undoubtedly even now there is still an acute housing shortage.'

He stopped reading. Was that a car drawing up? He went to the window. Yes, it was. Good. A uniformed chauffeur jumped smartly out and went to the rear door. He opened it and an elderly lady emerged. The judge waited without much hope to see if the superintendent followed her, but he did not. He did not really believe that an elderly lady was the something extraordinary, but nothing was impossible. She might have been Thompson's mother.

He went back to the paper. He was tired of the leading article. He would try the letters. They were at any rate shorter, some of them so short that he could really read the whole letter and follow it without his thoughts reverting to the superintendent.

'Sir,' he read, 'Mr Scudley-Brown has missed the point of my letter. If he will read the second sentence before the first he will find that he is mistaken.' Read the second sentence before the first? Then why didn't he write it first? How extraordinary. He must get the letter in question. Which date was it? The writer didn't say. Oh, well—it would all take up time. It couldn't be yesterday's.

The day before, perhaps. But why didn't he alter the order of the sentences in his original letter if they made easier sense that way? Extraordinary. That word again. How long would he be? Why did he have to leave Scotland Yard so late? After all, he was a High Court judge. He shouldn't be kept waiting, except for something urgent.

The bell rang. He went with deliberate slowness to open it. It was the postman, who couldn't get the only letter through the letter box. It was a packet on Her Majesty's Service containing the latest Acts of Parliament. He put it on his desk unopened, and went to look for the issue of *The Times* with the original letter in it. It really would be rather intriguing to see the letter. It wasn't in Monday's; the previous Saturday's then? No. Friday was almost a week ago. It must be in that. No, this is Thursday's. Where on earth is Friday's? He always kept them in the right place. Could he have taken it out and left it somewhere? He couldn't remember. He must look again. And then the bell rang and it was the superintendent.

'Come in and sit down, Superintendent,' he said. 'Cigarette?'

'Thank you, Sir Gerald. I will, if you don't mind.'

The superintendent took his time—what a time—in getting a cigarette out of the box offered to him and even longer to light it. He tried with his lighter without success. After several failures the judge offered a match.

'No, this works all right,' said the superintendent. 'Can't think what's happened to it today.'

He tried several more times, still without success.

Again the judge offered a match.

'I hate to give in,' said the superintendent. 'Lighters are rather like horses. If you let them know they're master, they'll be always playing you up.'

'Indeed?' said the judge. 'Did you train yours yourself?'

'Yes,' said the superintendent. 'Had it from a foal.'

'I suppose it has been fed?' said the judge.

He was amazed that he could talk with such apparent calm while the superintendent was wasting time with his beastly cigarette.

'Good gracious, Sir Gerald. You're quite right. I forgot to fill it. If I might have that match.'

The judge handed him the box. The superintendent broke the first match and the second went out, but with the third he was successful and he leaned back in his chair.

'Well,' said the judge, 'what's happened?'

'It's extraordinary,' said the superintendent.

'That's what you said before,' said the judge. 'What is it?'

'I've been to the War Office. Cedric Mattingly Wilson was discharged from the Army as unfit on the 18th February 1943.'

'There must be some mistake.'

'That's what I thought. I had the answer by telephone first. I couldn't believe it. So I went round myself. There's only one Cedric Mattingly Wilson in Army records. He has never been wounded, let alone killed, and he was discharged with an indifferent character on the day I mentioned. As far as Army records go, he is still alive.'

'But what about the school? They have him on the Roll of Honour.'

'That,' said the superintendent, 'is the next thing we must find out.'

CHAPTER TWENTY-SIX

The Headmaster Again

'Let's go at once,' said the judge, 'if you can manage it.'

'I'd already arranged to do so.'

'Good. What can the answer be? It's extraordinary.'

'Exactly what I said to you on the telephone, Sir Gerald.'

This reminded the judge of his uncomfortable twenty minutes, but his relief was sufficient to prevent him from being annoyed.

'As a matter of fact, I've telephoned the school and asked if the headmaster would see me at once. I didn't know at the time if you'd be able to come.'

'Did you speak to the headmaster himself?'

'It's odd you should say that, Sir Gerald,' said the superintendent. 'The man I spoke to obviously wasn't the headmaster but he said he was. Very strange I thought it. At a school, I mean.'

'As a matter of fact it was the headmaster,' said the judge.

'No, I assure you, Sir Gerald, it couldn't have been.'

'Wait till you meet him,' said the judge. 'You're going to have two surprises today.'

Then the judge explained. He did not think it fair to let the superintendent go through what he had been through, though he had to admit to himself how very much he would have liked to watch the performance.

The headmaster saw them immediately on their arrival.

'You're not going to arrest me, I hope,' he said. 'Anyway I plead not guilty and reserve my defence.'

'We've come on a very serious matter, Mr Sprout,' said the judge, 'and we'd be most grateful for your help.'

'Well,' said the headmaster, 'you never know when you may need the law, so I believe in keeping in with it.'

'You remember,' said the judge, 'that I asked you about Cedric Mattingly Wilson and you showed me from his record card that he was killed in the last war and then I saw his name on the War Memorial.'

'That's right,' said the headmaster. 'Someone left him some money and you want to find his widow?'

'No,' said the judge, 'nothing of the kind. What we want to know is where your school got the information about his death from.'

'Well, I wasn't here at the time, but I suppose they saw it in the casualty lists.'

'It was never in the casualty lists.'

'What d'you mean? The man's dead, isn't he?'

'Not so far as the War Office knows. They certainly have no record of his being killed. On the contrary he was discharged from the Army in 1943.'

'Crikey!' said the headmaster.

He rang the bell and Miss Pimple soon appeared.

'Pimple,' said the headmaster, 'have we still got the records from which they made up the casualty lists in the last war?'

'I'll see, sir,' said Miss Pimple, 'but it may take some time. They'll be stored away somewhere.'

'Get the boys on to it, Pimple. I want those records if we've got them.'

'What d'you think's happened?' he asked when Miss Pimple had gone.

'We've no idea,' said the judge. 'We only know that Mrs Burford says the man's alive and she's seen him. But she thought that he was recorded at the War Office as dead. She told us that this man Wilson told her and her husband that he'd slipped his identity disc on a dead soldier—you know the old story—and had been officially declared killed. Well, it's quite plain that he's not officially dead at the War Office, but he is here.'

'What may have happened,' said the superintendent, 'is that this chap Wilson, knowing that he'd been described as dead in the school magazine and that Burford knew that, spun the yarn about the identity disc. Naturally, he wouldn't expect anyone to check it up, as his name was on the War Memorial. And the Burfords believed it. As well they might.'

'And that,' said the judge, 'would account for their both being terrified to let us come to the school and at the same time declaring that the man was alive. But, first of all, we want to know how he came to be described as a dead man. Was it just a lucky accident for him, or what? Mistakes like that have occasionally occurred, particularly with common names like Wilson. His other names, of course, are far from common, but what happens is that X. Y. Wilson's name appears in the casualty list and by mistake they put the wrong one in the school magazine, and, as it suits the man in question, he lets the error be perpetuated, and invents the yarn about the identity disc to stop people making enquiries or just because he thought it a good story.'

'Oh, well,' said the headmaster, 'we can afford it. Our figures'll stand it.'

'Your figures?' queried the judge.

'Yes,' said the headmaster. 'If this means that Burford comes out and Wilson goes in, it adds one to the list. Burford was in it anyway with his six months.'

'What list?' asked the judge.

'If this had happened a few years back it'd have had me worried. Look, I'll show you.'

The headmaster pulled up a blind on the wall and showed them a table.

'Most schools,' he said, 'keep records of all the Prime
Ministers, Judges and Generals and so on they've
produced. Well, I keep a record of all the scallywags as
well. It isn't quite so easy to do because breaking and
entering doesn't always get reported, while being made
a Prime Minister does. So there are gaps in this list, but it
isn't bad. Have a look.'

It certainly was an imposing list.

'Personally,' he said, 'I think these lists should be
published. Then you could make a fair choice. You may
have a school where they've a wonderful record for
generals, but they've quite a good one for confidence
tricksters too. Well, you want to know, don't you? What
d'you want your son to be? If you want him to be an
undischarged bankrupt look at that one. There's the place
for him.'

He pointed to a school.

'It keeps up a good average, doesn't it? Been top of
this list for bankrupts for years. Only beaten once in the
last ten years. They must have a good economics master
there. Or it may just be tradition, just like some schools
are always good at one particular sport. Look at that one
for bigamy. Wonder who teaches them that.'

It really was an interesting table. Over fifty schools
were on the list and against each of them was their record
for the previous ten years for every kind of crime and for
bankruptcy. The judge looked for his school.

'Looking for yours?' said the headmaster. 'You'll find
it. How d'you like it? Now perhaps you'd like to see the
generals and the judges. Here.'

He went to another blind and lifted it up.

'There you are,' he said. 'You're on that. One judge
extra, whatever year that was. But, of course, you were
before we started the system. It isn't a bad idea, is it?
Look at this one. They got two knights that year. Now
look at the other table. Two housebreakers. Pretty well
cancels out. Don't suppose the knights were the house-

breakers. Of course they might have been. You'd know better than me about that.'

'No,' said the judge, 'most titled people who get convicted are charged with fraud or some financial swindle. Or murder, of course. There are no class distinctions there.'

'Sorry Pimple's taking so long,' said the headmaster, 'but it must be quite a business going back to 1943. This case of yours would have had me worried a few years back. We were neck and neck with St Willowbys. And one of their boys was charged with something. The trial took five days. It was like a test match here. If he was convicted, we were one up on them. If he was acquitted, we stayed equal. Then, just when things looked all right for us and the old judge was giving the defence hell—you know the way—if one of our boys wasn't charged with being drunk in charge of a car! We hardly did any work in the school that week I can tell you. But it was all right in the end. Our fellow got off and theirs got three years. But it was touch and go at one time. And if this case of yours had come up then, it'd have had me rattled. But it's all right now. We've gone ahead. They've had a couple of manslaughters and a bankruptcy to one fraud. They nearly had a murder too but they let the chap off. Juries getting a bit soft, don't you think?'

'They never like convicting if they can avoid it,' said the judge.

'That's your trouble, isn't it?' said the headmaster.

The judge went rather red.

'Certainly not,' he said, 'it's not our business to try to get a conviction.'

The headmaster whistled.

'Well,' he said, 'I've been to the Assizes, you know. Not one of our boys. Just to have a look. If the judge I saw wasn't working overtime to get the jury to convict, you can hang me too. And overtime's the right word, too. He was still at it at eight o'clock.'

'I can't agree with you at all,' said the judge. 'It's perfectly true that judges do sit a bit late sometimes in order to get through the work and personally I think that's undesirable in a criminal case. I never sit late myself except in civil cases and when there's no jury.'

'Well, I'm glad to hear it,' said the headmaster. 'But this man Burford you tried, why did the jury convict him if you were so keen on his getting off?'

'It was a very strong case on the face of it,' said the judge uncomfortably. 'It was only afterwards that I began to have doubts.'

'I see,' said the headmaster. 'Second thoughts best, eh?'

The judge was relieved that a moment later Miss Pimple returned.

'Good news, sir,' she said. 'We've found the records. Here you are. Cedric Mattingly Wilson, killed in action 23rd March 1943.'

'Yes, but how did the entry come to be made? His name isn't in the casualty lists,' said the judge.

'There's a letter here, sir, which I think gives the answer to that.'

She handed them a letter which read as follows:

Dear Sir,

I am sure you will be sorry to hear that my brother, Cedric Mattingly Wilson, was killed in action on the 23rd March 1943. As I have not seen his name in the School magazine I assume that you must have missed his name in the casualty lists. Please do not reply to this letter as I am staying with an aunt who sees all my letters and who was very much attached to my brother, and who has taken his death very badly. She is a little better at the moment but any mention of the matter now might set her back. I hope you will continue to send me my brother's copies of the magazine to the address you have and I enclose a further year's subscription.

Yours sincerely,
Richard Mattingly Wilson

The letter and address were typewritten.

'Is there nothing else?' asked the superintendent.

'Nothing as far as I can see,' said Miss Pimple. 'All the documents are here.'

They looked through them but could find nothing else.

'So what it comes to is this,' said the judge. 'This fellow Wilson, pretending to be his brother, writes a letter to the school magazine announcing his own death. The editor or headmaster has no reason to suspect its authenticity. What reason could a person have for making a false report? I suppose some very careful people would check with the War Office but that obviously didn't happen here and you can't blame them for not making a check. The address is probably a false address, very likely non-existent. Hence the request not to reply. But he wants the magazine to be sent in the ordinary way so that he can see if he's duly been entered as killed. As soon as he's got it, he becomes Thompson and invents the story of the identity disc. Anything wrong with that, Superintendent?'

'Depends what you mean by wrong, sir,' said the superintendent. 'But I'd like to take this letter if I may, sir. I'll give you a receipt for it. But somehow I think we shall owe Mrs Burford an apology. Of course, Burford's position isn't quite so clear. They might have been in it together. We shall have to go into that. But there's certainly a lot of work to be done on the case now. I'd better get straight back to the Yard.'

'I think,' said the judge, 'I shall call on Mrs Burford.'

'Well,' said the headmaster, 'very pleased to have been of some help. But, if you can help the school records by letting out Burford and not catching Wilson you'd be doing me a favour. No, don't look so unhappy. I don't mean it. You catch him. We haven't had a bank robber before and it'd be a pity to have to wash it out altogether.'

The judge and the superintendent, having thanked the headmaster and Miss Pimple for their help, hurried back to London. Lesley was in when the judge called on her.

'Have you come to arrest me?' she asked.

'I'm by myself,' he said, 'and we don't do our own arresting. No, I've come to apologise.'

'Apologise!'

Lesley jumped up excitedly.

'What's happened?' she said.

The judge told her.

'Then, when he told us that story of the identity disc, he was just telling lies?'

'Obviously. But he banked on your believing it, and nine people out of ten who'd seen his name in the school magazine would have done the same.'

'What'll happen now?'

'Well, I can't be sure,' said the judge, 'but I feel pretty certain that the police will now make an all-out attempt to find Thompson. So you'll be off to race-meetings again —but this time not with me.'

'You have been terribly kind,' said Lesley.

'I've been a mixture,' said the judge. 'But you mustn't start to get too excited. First of all they may never catch the man.'

'But you do believe me now about him?'

'Yes,' said the judge, 'I do. But, secondly, even if he is caught, we don't know what he'll say. A lot may depend on that. You see, your husband and he might have been in it together.'

'But, surely,' said Lesley, 'if you find William was telling the truth about the existence of Thompson, you'll believe him about the rest?'

'I can't answer for the Home Secretary, but I'm bound to say it should at the very least raise a serious doubt as to the justice of your husband's conviction.'

'That means they'll let him out?'

'I hope so,' said the judge, 'but it doesn't rest with me. And, I repeat, if Thompson is caught and implicates your husband, it must depend on what they both say.'

'But they must believe William after this. It would be so unfair not to.'

Two days later Lesley was being escorted all over the country to race-meetings by plain-clothes detectives. They had to go to more than six meetings before they found Mr Thompson, but they caught him in the end, and after they had taken his finger prints and found that they were the same as those found on the scene of the robbery he proved surprisingly co-operative. He made a complete confession entirely exonerating William and admitting that he'd deliberately tried to plant his crime on someone with a previous conviction and then telephoned the police to give them the tip. He said that he hoped that, once they'd got someone convicted, their search for the remainder of the gang would not be so active.

The reason for his co-operation became rather more obvious when, a few weeks after he had been in custody, he managed to escape from prison. The headmaster of his school was accordingly saved the sad task of adding one to the list of criminals. Confessions amount to nothing. You must be convicted before you go on the table. On the other hand it meant that the school had no bank robbers to its credit.

'Now, Spriggs,' said the headmaster, 'you'll have to get that Scholarship at Oxford to make up.'

CHAPTER TWENTY-SEVEN

Back to Work

WILLIAM was soon released and given a free pardon, but he was not awarded compensation. It was fairly pointed out that, if you tell lies to the police when enquiries are made of you, you have no right to complain if, in consequence, you are not only disbelieved but put in the dock and convicted.

The judge himself felt intensely relieved and he was congratulated by nearly all of his colleagues, particularly by those who had been most sceptical. Mr Justice Dalmunzie wrote him a short note.

'Well done,' it said. 'It seems that you could have safely left your bedroom door open.'

Term began again two days after William was released and the judge had an interesting session with himself the night before he was to sit at the Old Bailey. He felt he couldn't entirely blame himself for the Burford verdict. He had been grossly unfair, but, had he been fair, it would probably have made no difference to the verdict. But it was in consequence of his unfairness that he had suffered such appalling suspense and anxiety. He considered having a small notice to put in front of him with 'BE FAIR' on it, but, on the whole, he thought that would be inadvisable, as other people would see it. However, he did not really need a physical notice. It must surely now be so stamped on his mind that he could never forget it. And fortunately no harm had been done. On the contrary, probably, if he hadn't been unfair, William would have been convicted just the same and, much worse, served his

sentence. It was only because of his own unfairness that
the judge had taken the matter up. It was a pleasant
paradox. Burford owed his release to the judge being
unfair. But that was not to be used as a reason for being
unfair in the future. I wonder what case I shall first have
to try, he wondered. It would be a happy coincidence if
Empton were in it to see the difference.

Mr Empton *was* in it, defending a man on a simple
little charge of receiving cars knowing them to have been
stolen. The cars had arrived at the accused's yard without
number plates. The accused then proceeded to erase the
engine and chassis numbers and to spray the cars a
different colour. They were then handed back to the man
who had brought them. He was known to the accused as
Ernie. The accused did not ask Ernie where the cars came
from or why they had no number plates or why Ernie
wanted the numbers erased. He didn't think there was
anything wrong as Ernie seemed a 'genuine' person.

'Why,' he was asked by prosecuting counsel, 'do you
think Ernie wanted the numbers erased?'

'Never arst.'

'I know you never asked but why did you *think* he
wanted them erased?'

'It was 'is car, weren't it? 'E could do wot 'e liked with
it, couldn't 'e?'

Prosecuting counsel sat down and Mr Empton got up
to re-examine.

'Whatever Ernie may or may not have had in mind, did
you believe he was doing anything wrong?'

'Wot should I think he was doing anything wrong for?'

'So you didn't think,' said Mr Justice Carstairs, 'that
the man Ernie was doing anything wrong?' And he
looked at the jury with the look which Mr Empton knew
so well but still could not describe.